Sweet Spades
The Club Duology Book One

by

T.A. Torres

Sweet Spades

Contact Information: info@thewildrosepress.com

Cover Art by *Kristian Norris*

The Wild Rose Press, Inc.
PO Box 708
Adams Basin, NY 14410-0708

Visit us at www.thewilderroses.com

Publishing History
First Scarlet Rose Edition, 2019
Print ISBN 978-1-5092-2440-1
Digital ISBN 978-1-5092-2441-8

Published in the United States of America

Secrets, betrayal, and revenge come in spades…

How could this happen? I keep asking myself as I look across the green cloth table into the most piercing blue eyes I've ever seen. The man behind them is cold, dark, and void of emotion. He makes me wonder how someone so dangerous can be wrapped up into such a beautiful package.

"You going to fold, little girl?" He taunts me while we play. The corner of his kissable mouth curves up slightly, leaving me wanting to punch the smug, yet beautiful, grin off his face. I don't do it, though, because I know if I do, it might just be the very last thing I do. Plus, I need the money. That's what made me desperate enough to come willingly into the lion's den in the first place. I could literally kill my brother for getting himself thrown into jail.

Again.

I flip up the corner of my two cards that are face down on the table and peek at them. My face is straight and relaxed not giving any hint of an expression as I stare at the ace of hearts and the two of spades. Lying on the table face up is the king and queen of diamonds, two of hearts and a six of clubs. The game is Texas Hold'em, one that I have been familiar with since I was a young girl. Usually, I play for the thrill of the game. Tonight, I'm playing for much more than that.

Dedication

To Damian, I love you more. I win :p

A woman once said a man is like a deck of playing cards; you need the heart to love him, a diamond to marry him, a club to bash his fucking head in, and a spade to bury the bastard.—Unknown

Chapter One

Kylie

How could this happen? I keep asking myself that as I glance across the green cloth table into the most piercing blue eyes I have ever seen. The man behind them is cold, dark, and void of emotion. He makes me wonder how someone so cruel can be wrapped up in such a beautiful package.

"Are you going to fold, little girl?" He taunts me while we play. The corner of his kissable mouth curves up, slightly, making me want to punch the smug, yet perfect grin on his face. I wouldn't dare touch him though, attempting to do so is foolish, and I pride myself on being smarter than that.

I flip up the corner of my two cards, lying face down on the table, and peek at them, clearing my throat. I relax my body, locking away any hint of expression that could give me away. My empty clutch sits on the table to my right, reminding me why I came willingly into the lion's den in the first place.

Money.

I'm desperate for cash. Twenty thousand dollars in

fact, which would be about enough to bail my brother, Tyler, out of jail. Once I do get him out, I might kill him for forcing me into my current situation. Playing poker against one of Chicago's most prominent crime bosses.

I continue to stare at the ace of hearts and two of spades in my hand. The king and queen of diamonds, two of hearts, and six of clubs are still on the table between us. The game we're playing is Texas Hold'em. One of the many card games I've been familiar with since I was a young girl with a father who was addicted to gambling. After years of poker, I mostly just chased the thrill, but with my brother's freedom on the line, there is a lot at stake tonight. The need to leave here with my pockets full is the same as my next breath. Unfortunately, the pair of twos I've been dealt isn't going to win me anything at all, and by the look of the grin plastered across my competitor's face, he knows he's got this round in the bag.

I narrow my eyes at him. "No, I'm not going to fold." My voice comes out steady and confident, leaving myself surprised. "Are you?" My brow raises in question.

He shakes his head. "Let me do you a favor." His voice is rough and masculine when he speaks; he demands attention.

The room is silent around us. The only noise in the entire place comes from the disgusting man in a suit sitting to his right, heavily breathing while sucking down a cigar. The cloud of smoke he exhales creates a thin layer of fog that I find myself embracing like a shield, hiding me from the man who sits across from me until the smoke clears leaving me vulnerable again.

"You aren't exactly known for handing out favors to anyone." I keep my lips straight. This is not my first time playing poker, nor is it my first time at an underground club. I try to convince myself it also isn't my first time around a powerful, intimidating, gorgeous man, but that is a lie. He is like no one I have ever met before.

He doesn't fit the average profile of a card shark. The ones I have spent years dealing with were old enough to be my father, some even the age of my grandfather. They always reminded me of characters in mobster movies. Older Italian men dressed in suits, wearing pinky rings with hair that had been grayed out from years of stress and experiences.

I take in the man in front of me; he has to be at very least six feet tall, his shoulders are broad, arms roped with muscles. His eyes, which I noticed first about him, are a shocking blue that pulls me in right away. His hair is dark brown, and his complexion is tan, as if he just walked right off a cruise ship hours ago. Every single detail about him screams, "panties melt right off women when I enter a room." I would know. I practically felt mine trying to escape my body at first sight of him.

He's dressed in a white button-down shirt with both the sleeves rolled up to his elbows. His muscular forearms are in view, one of them shows off a full tattoo sleeve with various shades of dark gray and black. From my seat, it appears to be demons and angels sketched into his skin. It looks dark, yet beautiful at the same time, perfect for the man wearing them. The tattoo continues on the one side of his chest, leaving a few lines running up his collarbone and neck.

3

The desire to reach out and trace the lines of them courses through me. I shake the lousy thought from my head.

"For you, I'm feeling generous. You've managed to beat everyone else in here tonight; it's the least I can do." He gives me a dangerous smile, while his eyes lock into mine. I slowly follow them run down from my face to my C cup-sized chest that is currently pouring out of the low cut, tight, black dress I'm wearing.

I chose this dress for a reason, and the hungry look in his eyes says it is serving its purpose. By the time he brings his eyes back up to mine, goosebumps have broken out on my skin, my nipples are tight, and every part of my body is humming. If I didn't feel nervous enough before, I'm practically crawling out of my skin now. His gaze is intense. Everything about him is harsh, dangerous, and hot.

I find myself refusing to buy into anything he is offering, no matter how tempting he may be. People always say the devil was once beautiful. Plus, there is the fact that nothing in life comes without cost. I've learned that the hard way in the past. All it takes is one glance at him for me to suffocate from the mysterious air coming off him. There's not a chance I would consider making a deal with him and still expect to come out on top.

My hands tighten around my cards. I'm going to let this play out. My brothers are worth the risk. Tyler and his twin Chase have spent the majority of their lives taking care of me. After our mom passed away from cancer and our father took off, they were the ones who stepped up and took over. I can't imagine how hard it had to be for two boys, who grew up on the wrong side

4

of the tracks, to raise a younger girl. Still, they always found a way to do what they could to make me happy, and because of that, I'll forever feel indebted to them. We are all each other has left in this world, and we stick together, through thick and through thin.

On top of that, I don't trust this man for shit, which makes the decision a no brainer. He doesn't seem like the type to do anything without an ulterior motive, and I have zero desire to be indebted to him. Cutting a deal with him would be like sacrificing myself to the devil. "I can't do that," I finally tell him, refusing his offer.

He nods, wearing a smug grin, then slides the last card face down in front of me. "I'll allow you to look at the card that will determine your fate, first."

This card needs to be another two. Which would leave me with three of a kind and my last hope at a chance of walking out of here with the cash. Sadly, that isn't even a hand to write home about. Looking across the table, I watch as he flips up the corner of his two-hole cards again. A slow smile takes over his face, transforming him from handsome to downright sexy. He brings his sharp eyes back up to me and crosses his arms over his chest. Casually, he leans back in his chair, without a care in the world. I admire him for a second, forgetting the gravity of the situation I'm in.

Awareness slowly creeps back into me. My stomach drops, and I let out a frustrated breath, pushing out all the air in my lungs. My hand goes up to my neck, tugging at my cross chain, pulling it away from me because it started feeling too tight. The feeling begins to consume me; panic starts to rise in my throat I keep breathing frantically, the atmosphere suddenly becomes overwhelming. I'm aware he has me beat, and

I haven't even looked at the river card yet. After I gain control of my body and the courage to peek at my card, staring back at me is the jack of spades. I let out another annoyed breath. The jack of fucking spades is still staring back at me laughing because that is what I'll be walking out of here with. Jack shit.

Lowering both of my hands to the arms of the chair I'm sitting in, I use them to push my body up physically. Without the support of them, I would most likely collapse onto the ground. Fighting the urge to run out of the club and far away from this man, I stand tall with my head held high. I prefer to walk out with some dignity still intact.

I don't even bother to see what the cocky bastard has in his hands. I have no desire to give him any more satisfaction. The last thing I expected was to come in here and lose.

The beginning of the night was spent with me up a few thousand dollars. After getting a few Cosmos in me, I was genuinely having a good time flirting with the suckers around me, while taking their money. Guilt never hit me for hustling them. Then this gorgeous man made his way down from the VIP area. The atmosphere in the entire place shifted as he descended the stairs. The women stopped and admired as the men sat up straighter. Control and dominance clung to him like a second skin, making the entire place go still. Once he sat down across from me, recognition hit me like a ton of bricks, and at that moment, I knew it was game over for me.

"Miss Turner?"

My name rolls off his lips causing me to pause for a second and look into his cold eyes. The sound of his voice calling my name sends shivers up my spine. I never told this man my name, and that doesn't sit right with me. I should have known he would know my name, and the names of every other degenerate gambler in here. This is his kingdom, after all. Internally I curse myself. Out of all the clubs of Chicago, I had to walk into his tonight.

"Sit back down. I didn't dismiss you yet." His voice stern, he smacks his palms flat on the table.

I pause, taking a quick glance around the room, considering my options. There's a massive, armed man at the front door. His stance screams military or maybe something darker, not a chance I'm getting past him. Even if I were to, the two men standing behind him, casually resting their hands on the top of the guns they have strapped on, might shoot me. Now if by some miracle I managed to get through the front door, I doubt I would make it across the street without one of them catching me.

Letting out a frustrated sigh, I turn my attention back to Asher's angry glare. He shakes his head silently, telling me no, like he knew what I was thinking. I slowly lower myself back into my chair as he dismisses the crowd around us. Without any words exchanged, people fumble out of the area as if there was a fire about to engulf us. Looking around I try to catch the eye of someone to stay and help me out; my wish goes unanswered as everyone avoids me like the plague. Finally, I'm left alone at the table with him. The lion and the gazelle.

"Don't ever think about running away from me again. For one, you won't get far, and even if you did, I would find you in the morning." His words are laced with venom, and I would be a fool to think he didn't mean every one of them. I'm in his world; this is his show.

"I wasn—"

He shoots up out of his chair before I can even finish my sentence. Crouching over the table, he cages me in with his hands gripping onto the armrests of my chair. The same chair arms I used to support myself earlier are now keeping me caged in. His face is so close to mine I can almost feel the anger coming off him.

"Don't lie to me." His stance is menacing over my body, the vein in his neck visibly ticks.

I flinch on instinct and swallow hard, feeling a lump caught in my throat. I've managed to poke the beast. I do nothing. I say nothing. I'm not even sure I'm breathing at this point. He is a criminal. He kills people, and not only have I thought about running from him, but I've also been caught trying to lie my way out.

Finally, he backs away entirely composing himself, as if he didn't send fear rocketing straight through my body. "Now that we have settled that, I know why you came here tonight, and I am going to offer you another way to make that twenty thousand dollars."

My eyes widen. "How?"

"How what? How do I know your one brother has landed himself in jail? How do I know that the other one is fighting underground as we speak? Or how will you earn money?"

"All of it?" Except the last part because I will not be making any deal with someone like you." I'm not that stupid, even though the actions that lead up to this very moment say otherwise.

His hand goes to his chest. "Someone like me? I'm insulted." He smiles amused for a second before his face grows serious again. "The answer is simple. I know every single thing that goes on in this city."

He does. I grew up hearing stories about the infamous Asher Black. He has his hands in every illegal activity in all of Chicago. He's also been in and out of jail for most of his life, yet only convicted once for possession of a weapon. Such a petty thing to go down for considering all his other crimes.

Growing up on the rougher side of town as I did, a man like him becomes a legend. I try not to believe the stories. For the most part, I thought they were bullshit, but being here, seeing the man in person, I'd put money on them all being real. That is if I had any money left. What am I going to do?

His voice pulls me out of my thoughts. "I am offering to bail your brother out of jail."

"What?" My mouth drops open. That sure as hell was the last thing I was expecting. "Why would you want to do that? You don't even know me."

"Kylie Turner, age twenty-four, went to a community college and graduated with a degree in teaching. Currently, you teach at the middle school at the end of Fourteenth Street. You and your two older brothers sure did make a name for yourselves. Tyler, the mechanic with more stolen cars on his lot then actual customer owned ones. Then we have Chase, who is undefeated in the underground fighting ring. My personal favorite of the three is you." He stops, sending a wink in my direction before continuing. "The sweet little innocent blonde, but that's not all you are since your hobbies include hustling guys at the poker table in casinos or illegal establishments, such as this one. Did I miss anything?" He finishes looking down at his watch as if my presence was a bore.

"Holy crap, stalk much?"

"No, I like to know all my criminals, and you and your brothers fit the category." He shrugs, calling over a waitress carrying drinks. He grabs a glass of amber liquid then sends her away before offering me anything. *I get it. This isn't a friendly exchange.*

I want to tell him I'm not a criminal, but at this point, that would be pointless, being where I currently am and all. "So, you're just going to bail my brother out of jail out of the kindness of your heart?" I shake my head, raising a brow. "Because that I don't believe for one second."

He smiles, and like a magnet, my attention is drawn back to his perfect mouth. "Of course the fuck not. In exchange, you're going to stay with me, live in my house, and sleep in my bed. Until I say otherwise."

What. The. Actual. Hell. This man is obviously gorgeous; he can get any woman he wants. He has money, not exactly clean money, but does a cashier give a damn where the money comes from? He is also feared by pretty much everyone in this entire state, possibly country, and I'm just a petty gambler. I used to think I was a good one at that, but since he beat me, I'm beginning to rethink my skill.

"Ha! Yeah, I'm going to need some of the drugs that you're on. Not happening. Goodbye, Mr. Black." I get up again pushing my chair back, ready to leave.

"Sit back down, Kylie." His hand reaches out and wraps around my bicep. He applies just enough pressure, so I'm aware that he is in control, but not enough to hurt me. "You don't have much of choice here."

"I do. I'll figure out how to get the money. Anything is better than having to live with you and your delightful personality." I inch in closer to his face till I can feels his angry breath on my lips.

The asshole laughs then backs away. He reaches for his drink with his free hand, finishing it in one gulp before slamming it down. "Good luck. You came in here because you needed me. You just didn't know it yet."

My anger swells inside of me, ready to burst out and lash at him. I try to pull my arm back. His grip tightens. "Screw you," I spit at him.

"Is that an invitation, doll? Why else do you think I want you in my house and my bed?"

I see red. "Are you serious? You're going to spend twenty grand to get my brother out of jail so that you can fuck me?"

He laughs again, like my anger is nothing other than a child throwing a tantrum over a broken toy, which pisses me off even more. I look around the room, trying to gain control of my anger. People send curious glances in my direction, but their eyes don't linger long before pulling away.

"I make twenty grand in the amount of time it takes me to take a piss. Don't let it get to your head."

"I have a boyfriend, you arrogant prick."

The minute the words fly out of my mouth, I regret them. Asher's lips grow tight, nostrils flaring. He tightens his grip on my arm and begins walking, dragging me through the club. I try making eye contact with anyone in the crowd, pleading for someone to help me out. My pleas go unanswered once again as the group turns their heads in the opposite direction. He continues pulling me around until we are alone in a back room, leaving the people and poker tables behind. Finally, he lets me go and I back away instantly, putting as much distance as I can between us.

Taking in my surroundings, I notice we are standing in what once was a bar. Most of the original furniture sits still in its place as if nothing has been disrupted in years. The musty smell causes me to wonder how long ago this place went out of business. The pool table in the center has a cover over it with a layer of dust sitting on top. Absently, I run my fingers over it, then brush away the sheet of film it left on my fingertip. I turn my back around toward Asher.

He stares at me intensely. His breathing is heavy as he struggles to reel his anger back in. "I don't give a damn what you tell that asshole cop you've been screwing. It should be easy enough for you since you've been lying to him for years about what you've been up to every weekend."

Catching me off guard, he proves again that he does know everything. I rest my hip against the pool table behind me; I'm calmer now oddly enough in a room alone with him.

"I need to think about it," I finally tell him, knowing without a doubt why I'm even considering this crazy deal. My brothers are my life, and there is absolutely nothing I wouldn't do for them. Simple as that. They have made a ton of sacrifices for me through the years. They made sure I was up and ready for school every morning and that I had a ride home after. I can't even think about the number of hours they spent cursing at each other over homework that I couldn't figure out on my own. Then together they raised enough money to put me through college. I never asked about the things they must have pulled and the risks they took to give me a better life. They are everything to me.

Casually, he crosses his arms over his broad chest and leans against the bar. "No, you have five minutes to decide before the offer is off the table. The more time you waste, the longer your brother has to protect his ass in jail."

I narrow my eyes at him, utterly hating him for playing me like this. If looks could kill, Asher Black would be drowning in a pool of his blood at my feet. "When you put it that way, what choice does it give me?"

He isn't the slightest bit fazed. "Glad we have a deal. Tyler will be a free man in the morning. I will have a car pick you up by eight tomorrow night." He waves dismissing me.

Just like that, I'm walking out of the club as fast as possible with my pride and dignity left behind on the table, and a deal made with the devil.

Chapter Two

Asher

I watch Kylie practically run out of my club. She's a smart girl by trying to get the hell away from me as fast as she can. I can't give her much credit for coming here in the first place, though. To say I was shocked when she walked through my doors is an understatement. She hadn't a clue that I knew who she is and who her scumbag boyfriend is.

I stood watching her from the tinted window of my private room above the poker tables. She was a sight to see in a short black dress and fuck me black pumps. My cock jumped watching her bend over the table making her tits bounce, while the men she was playing against looked like they were under a spell. Maybe she does deserve some credit. She did have them distracted while she took their money.

I fought myself to stay where I was and let her leave. Let her go home and wait for her piece of a shit cop to get off his shift and go to her. If I was a better person, I might have done just that, but I'm not. I couldn't let this opportunity slip away from me; hell, maybe it was fate that brought her here in the first place tonight. Who knows?

Just as I was about to make my way down to her, she looked up and locked eyes with me through the window. I knew she couldn't see who I was, but she knew I was there staring back at her. With that, the decision was made. It was time for me to make my move.

Recognition hit her face as soon as I sat at the table across from her. Everyone knows who I am or at least have heard of my name. With my mugshot plastered on the television and in the newspapers, it's hard not to be recognized. She even grew up in the neighborhood I did, and people talk. I could see the fear hit her big green eyes the moment I took the seat across from her.

I taunted her while we played. She held her own against me. Honestly, I was impressed with her, and no one ever impresses me. I watched her when she would get nervous. She tried to mask her face from me, but I could still see the disappointment in her eyes. How she's been lying to her asshole cop without him suspecting anything is a fucking mystery to me.

Maybe my conscious kicked in when I offered her a deal to walk away. I tried to intimidate her, but her face turned a shade of pink, and her breathing hitched when I ran my gaze from her eyes down to her barely covered rack. Thoughts ran through my mind, the moment I saw the desire in her eyes. *Take the offer and never come back in here or any other club. I will ruin you if you don't accept.* When she finally refused, I knew just how desperate she must be to bail her brother out. I had no idea her loyalty ran this deep. I nodded instantly pleased knowing I had her where I wanted her.

I slid our last card across the table, for her to reveal, and she instantly went still, knowing this was her last hope. I looked at my two cards again, and I couldn't help the smile spreading across my lips. I knew she was waiting on a third deuce, and I also knew that wasn't the river card, or last card, dealt. I didn't make it this far in life not knowing what is going on around me. She was good, but I was better. My body relaxed. I lounged back in my chair letting the confidence pour out of me, thick enough for her to feel it. She needed to know it wasn't a game I ever intended on losing.

After what felt like a century later, Kylie lifted the corner of the card. She never asked to see what I had, and she knew I already won. Anger and frustration passed through her face. Her nose scrunched up, and as much of a pussy as it makes me sound like, I have to admit, it was kind of cute.

The thought passed quickly; my eyes grew cold when she tried to stand up and walk away. I gave her that chance already, and she foolishly declined. No fucking way was she walking away now.

"Miss Turner." I raised my voice as I said her name.

She instantly paused, then looked around like she was ready to flee. How amusing, she thought she could run from me. I shook my head at her trying to keep things as civil as possible. In her hasty attempt to get away, her card flipped over to reveal a jack of spades. Life can be funny, yet cruel sometimes.

I lost it the second she began to deny it. I was out of my chair and in her face. She thought she could lie to me. I had given her an opportunity to leave. That's more than others can say I've done for them. Then she had the balls to lie to me in my own club.

I composed myself as an idea crossed my mind that would benefit both me and my cock. I smile to myself thinking about how it went down. I had Kylie right where I wanted her, and just like a hungry fish, she took the bait.

"Jimmy," I call my head of security over.

"Yeah, boss." He walks over, stopping in front of me, the scar lining the side of his face visible without the usual hat he wears.

"Follow her home, and make sure she gets in. I have to go take a little trip to the pig pen." I laugh, knowing what I am about to do is going to piss her pig officer off.

Chapter Three

Asher

"Well shit, I never thought I would see the day Asher Black would walk into the police station without cuffs around his wrist." And that is why there is nothing worse than a cop; they are all entitled pricks.

"Officer Owens, so thrilled to see you." My tone drips sarcasm as I look at the man before me. He's my exact match in height and weight, but that's about the only similarity we share, well appearance wise anyway. His arms are crossed over his chest. I take in his nameplate reading "Owens" and shake my head in disgust. Hard to believe I was ever close to this asshole, but that ship has long sailed then crashed and burned somewhere in the Bermuda Triangle.

"What are you doing here, Ash?" His head tilts to the side, curiously, his eyes sizing me up.

I cringe on the inside when he calls me Ash. He did it on purpose. He's waiting to get a reaction out of me, but I don't give him one. I haven't been Ash to him or anyone else in a long time. Ash is gone. All that is left is Asher. "I'm here to let you know I'll be bailing out an old friend."

"Who?" officer asshole asks.

"Tyler Turner." I try to hide my grin. I know this is going to eat at him. "You may know of him."

He takes a step closer to me and stops a few inches

away from my face. He's close enough so that I can see the vein in his neck throbbing. I watch every police officer in the station begin to close in on us, ready to step in before all hell breaks loose as if I'm stupid enough to hit a cop with these many witnesses surrounding me in a fucking police station no less. Assholes.

"Why would you bail him out?" His brows draw together, his breathing heavies.

"I think the better question would be why you are not bailing him out?" I taunt him. I shouldn't, but this is too good to stop. He is livid; it's clear as day to me. I know him better than anyone here. "Is it not his little sister who is keeping your dick wet at night?"

The jerk officer is about ready to hit me, and I welcome it. I want to see that he isn't the pussy I know he is. He's struggling to keep his composure, but nothing comes just like I expected as he sighs and takes a step back, throwing his hands in the air. "This city doesn't pay me to bail out the criminals." I already learned the hard way when he left me to rot in a jail cell for a year.

"Good thing I'm here then, right?" I ask, sarcastically.

Officer Owens gives me a hard stare narrowing his eyes, "What game are you playing here?"

I smile back. "Goodnight, Officer." I emphasize the officer part because that is all he is to me now. Just another cop in a town run by criminals.

"Shit," Officer Owens whispers.

I walk out the door of the police station. If he thinks bailing out Kylie's brother is wrong, then he has no clue what I plan on doing to his little liar.

I'll admit the situation is disastrous. Kylie will be an innocent casualty in a game that she is entirely unaware of. She's about to be thrown head first in the middle of a war between her boyfriend and me. I wish that was enough to stop me, but it's not.

Compassion and guilt are emotions I left behind a long time ago. There aren't many good redeeming qualities left inside of me if any at all.

She came to me; she walked through my doors. I didn't hold a gun to her head. She made the deal with me on her own free will. One wrong decision that will ruin her, but it's all because of her boyfriend not because of my attraction toward her; I remind myself.

In my defense, this was never part of my plan, to begin with, but when she strolled in with her tight black dress and long blonde hair that stopped just below her ample rack, I knew what I was going to do.

She is gorgeous. Her bright green eyes drew me in, and I'm only a man after all. I would have to be blind not to want her.

It took a lot out of me not to bend her over the musty old pool table in that back room when she was throwing her attitude around. That wouldn't have helped my case though; I'll have her, but not yet. I'll make sure she begs for me before I take her.

A smile tugs my mouth, for once it seemed like shit was finally going my way. She made the mistake of coming to me, and she will regret it, but not before I have my fun.

My burner phone vibrates in my pocket. "Boss." Jimmy's voice comes through.

"What is it?"

"You aren't going to be happy, but your girl is

making her way to the Pit."

I snap my phone shut, taking one last drag of my cigarette, before putting it out on the faded bricks of the old police station. It looks like I'm in for a long night.

Chapter Four

Kylie

I push my way through the crowd at the Pit, wishing I had stopped home and changed before coming. Instead, I'm making my way through sweaty male bodies in a barely there dress. The sound of my pumps clicks off the cement floor has heads turning in my direction. Rolling my eyes, I continue the search for my brother.

The Pit is a gruesome and barbaric place that a woman should never step foot in alone. Lucky for me, everyone knows who I am, and who my brothers are, so other than the occasional catcall, nobody messes with me.

Taking in the dingy and utterly bare basement, I can see the blood stained into the concrete floors from the decades of men who've fought here. I shiver at the sight. The stench of sweat and overused cheap cologne fills my nose. Nothing can prepare me for that smell. The men who come here to watch, scream, curse, and cheer don't notice how disgusting this Pit is. Honestly, even if they did, they wouldn't care. They are only here for the thrill. I'd imagine it's similar to the rush I get while at a poker table. I can almost feel the excitement in the air as people place money on who they believe is the stronger fighter. Unfortunately doing so, they don't give one single damn about who gets hurt in the process. They cheer louder when more blood is spilled. I shake my head in disgust and continue looking around.

I finally spot him in the center of all the people that are already cheering around him, pumping him up even more. The adrenaline pouring through the basement is electric. I'm sure there is a lot of money riding on Chase's victory tonight.

After years of coming here to watch my brother Chase fight, I still get that sick feeling in my stomach every time. He has a big match tonight, and if he wins the payout is five grand. Our plan was for both of us to do what we know and earn money to bail Tyler out. The desperation for cash forced us into this. Isn't money always the cause for desperate measures? At least there is still a chance for me to stop him now that we don't need the cash. But he's a hot head, and talking him out isn't going to change his mind. He will never back down from a fight and ruin the reputation he fought hard for. With his pride on the line, there isn't a chance in hell he would walk away.

I make my way over to him. He has his shirt off, and two girls in bikinis hanging off him. The one bimbo on his right has gigantic boobs that look ready to bust out of the tiny piece of cloth concealing them. The other one I recognize as a girl I went to high school with, Stella. She has a reputation a mile long. Rumor has it she's been drinking and smoking since the second grade. Rolling my eyes at the sight before me, I can't even say I'm the least bit surprised to see them hanging on him fighting for his attention. Little do they know that he will spend a night with each, maybe even at the same time, then never talk to them again.

He can be such a cocky asshole sometimes, and it shows from looking at him. Both Chase and his twin, Tyler, are tall and broad, with a charm that knocks panties off women. They aren't identical, but both share my blonde hair. Chase was blessed with the same green eyes as me, while Tyler has our father's brown eyes. Physically, Chase has bulkier muscle due to his lifestyle choice, while Tyler has more lean muscle. They are both genuinely handsome. Sometimes, I wish they weren't. I've spent many nights with my head under the pillow, trying to drown out the sounds of the different women they bring home. Too many times, I've watched them shuffling random ones out in the morning.

I remember one time Chase made me storm into his room and play the role of an angry girlfriend because the girl wouldn't leave. Despite how much I screamed at her and him, the dumb girl still wouldn't take the hint. Tyler and I laugh about that one to this day.

"How'd it go, Kye?" Chase calls out to me over the noisy crowd once he spots me. Both girls take me in from head to toe before shooting me a glare. *Put your claws away, ladies. I'm no threat here.*

"It went," I yell back without elaborating, my eyes dart around the room avoiding eye contact with him. "You don't need to fight."

I can't possibly be vaguer, but this isn't the time or the place for me to tell him about my night. He is going to flip his lid when I tell him what I've agreed to do. Saying that he and Tyler are protective of me is an understatement. The problem is Chase is more unpredictable, like a bull in a china shop. He has always lived his life by acting first then thinking later. Which is the reason it's crucial Tyler is out as soon as possible, because somebody needs to keep him in line, and that is a full time job that I want zero part in. Crazy to think that Tyler would be the one arrested in the first place.

I'll never forget getting the call from my boyfriend, Blake, informing me that my brother had been taken in on charges of grand theft. Chase was standing beside me fuming, trying to rip the phone from my hand. The cops caught Tyler in a brand new sports car in a neighborhood with fountains made of gold, cobblestone streets, and mansions the size of Texas. Chase thinks the cops were following him that night. Tyler has been boosting cars for years, never once getting caught. I tried countless times begging him to stop, but like Chase, he never listened to me. Thankfully, it wasn't Blake who arrested him. He was calling to give me the heads up and to tell us to meet him at the station. Had it been Blake who arrested Tyler, Chase might have been sharing a cell with him for murder.

"I'm fighting." Chase turns his attention back to the big boobs on his right, smiling at her.

My lip pulls up in disgust. "Please don't fight." My words fall on deaf ears as the announcer makes his way toward the center of the circle the crowd has made. I take the time to peek over at Chase's opponent. The man, or should I say, giant, standing across from him is beyond freaking huge. My stomach drops at the sight of him; nervous anxiety starts to take over as I wipe my sweaty hands on my dress.

"To my right; at six feet, two inches tall, weighing two hundred and seventy-five pounds, is Chase, the tank, Turnerrrrr!" The crowd goes nuts as the announcer's voice fills the smoky air. "And his opponent to my left standing at six feet, five inches, weighing three hundred and twenty pounds, Hunter the hellhound, Lloydddd!" Loud boos break out from every direction. I hear someone scream, "Kill him, Tank" then the chanting begins around us. "Kill him, Tank."

My adrenaline is at an all-time high as Chase closes in on his opponent. He strikes fast and powerful, drawing blood the first punch he lands across Hunter's jaw. Hunter's head flies back for a brief second before he spits out blood, then smiles. Crazy lunatic. Chase doesn't slow down or stop his assault for a second. He attacks like a caged animal.

He has had practice for this moment his entire life; it's the only way he knows. Each blow Chase throws at his opponent is more powerful than the last. Hunter hits the ground with a loud thump. The bigger they are, the harder they fall. Chase always tells me he prefers his opponents larger than him. The smaller ones are faster and being over six feet makes them harder for him to catch.

Blood is pouring from Hunter's face. He's lying on the ground crouched over and cradling his one side. The only way the fight is over is by a knockout. Hunter is still conscious. If he can pull himself up the match will continue. *Stay down. Stay down.*

Chase struts around the circle, taunting him, making the crowd cheer louder. He's too busy being a jackass to notice the man in the hoodie approaching Hunter on the ground. I watch him try to help Hunter get up. He's holding something in his hand. I push myself forward through the bodies trying to make out the object he's driving toward Hunter to take. It's when I catch a reflection of light coming off a metal object; I begin to panic.

"Chase!" I scream, knowing he can't hear me over the crowd's hollers. I look back up as the hooded man retreats into the sea of people until he's entirely out of sight.

"Chase!" I scream again frantically. I try to jump over the people in my way. I'm pushing and hitting whoever gets in front of me. My only focus is to get to him and warn him. A sick feeling settles in my stomach as I watch Hunter barrel toward Chase with the knife in his hand. Then all hell breaks loose.

Someone screams "knife" causing everyone to scatter in different directions. My body is pushed around, like a rag doll, farther and farther away from my destination. I curse myself again for the stupid stinking heels I wore tonight.

"Chase! Chase!" I desperately continue to scream. I lose complete sight of him as people are yelling, and fights begin to break out all over. I'm determined to get to my brother to make sure he's okay, but instead, I'm stuck fighting my way through the chaos that has erupted.

I catch sight of my brother's opponent, Hunter, through the crowd, and his eyes lock with mine. The moment sucks me in. Everything goes still. It's as if we are the only two people in the room. Blood is dripping down a large gash in his head, pouring down onto his bare chest. He winks and smiles his red stained teeth at me, before turning around and retreating into the crowd. I'm angry and disgusted. I would love to do nothing more than take his knife and shove it into his black heart.

More screaming and chaos pull me out of the spell. I start heading toward the direction the hooded man disappeared from, clinging to the thought of killing him till I can feel my hands going numb at my sides from clenching my fists so tight. My body is wound up on adrenaline. I'm ready to take that mother on.

I make it not even a foot in his direction until I'm stopped by strong arms wrapping around my waist, then my back is pulled into a hard body. I squirm, using all my strength trying to break free. "No! Get off me!" I scream, struggling against my capture's arms.

"No, Kylie," he says into my ear. I know that voice even through all the chaos around me I can recognize that voice anywhere. I just sold my soul to him earlier tonight for a whopping twenty thousand dollars.

I relax I know he won't hurt me. Oddly enough, I feel safe in the arms of the city's biggest criminal. "Asher, I need to find Chase, let me go," I plead, as his grip tightens around me. The energy of tonight is beginning to drain from my body; I fall more into his solid chest. His body feels warm and hard; his muscular arms wrapped around me. My heart starts calming down. I feel safe, for the first time tonight.

He grins against my ear. "Is that where you just were about to go? Or did you think you were going to run after that walking steroid with a knife? Tell me, my sweet Spade."

Spade? What the hell? Then it dawns on me the last card I was dealt, the card that changed everything, the jack of spades.

Asher scoops my legs from underneath me, lifting me up, and pressing me against his chest. He cradles me, holding me tight against his body like I am no more than a tiny baby. People stop pushing and fighting around us and watch in amazement. A path clears out in the direction he begins walking. It's like Moses parting the Red Sea as people retreat from the murderous glare on his face. People know him. The man pours out dominance. There are traces of fear in the faces of people who back away from us. From him.

I feel like I'm in a dream that none of tonight happened, or maybe I'm in a nightmare. I haven't decided which, yet. The cold night air hitting my face and the sound of the city traffic pull me back into the reality of what went down. The city is buzzing around us as I'm held tightly in Asher Black's arms, carried out of harm's way. I'm not sure how I feel about it as I try to squirm out of his grasp again. I still want to get back inside and look for my brother. If anything happened to him, I would… I can't even finish that thought.

Asher holds me tighter carrying me into the back seat of his limo. Once inside, he sits with me on his lap. I try to get up, but his arms wrap back around me as he pulls me down against his hard chest. There isn't much fight left in me. I allow him to hold me. He rubs his hands through my hair comforting me. Even if I had the strength to pull away from his grasp, physically I am no match for him.

"To Miss Turner's house, Jimmy." He calls to his driver, who I notice is also the same huge man who was at his club guarding the front door. The very one I foolishly debated running past. It's hard to believe that was only a few hours ago. It feels like it was days ago.

Chapter Five

Kylie

Asher Black is sitting at my kitchen table. He looks out of place in the small two-bedroom house that my brothers and I grew up in. I would imagine he could fit three of my homes in his bathroom alone. Right now, I don't give a crap if it doesn't live up to his standards. He hasn't said anything to hint toward that, but I'm sure the man who can buy anything in the world is thinking it.

I pace as he watches me. My brothers and I have always had a plan to meet again at the house if things ever go to shit. They have drilled the escape route into my head since I was young girl and didn't understand what we needed one for. Tonight I'm grateful for it knowing that Chase will get here. It was as if Asher knew this all along when he told his driver to take us here. He would know all about escape plans, probably better than anyone else.

I keep assuming the worst happened, and I wasn't able to reach him. Nothing can bring out fear of seeing a crazed man go after your family member with a knife. Never once have I seen someone try something like that in the Pit. It was a desperate and coward move. I think back to the smile he gave me. I had to go after him. I was determined to catch him. Good thing for Asher to step in. I was no match for a man like Hunter. I would never admit my gratitude to Asher, though.

"You're going to burn a hole in the floor if you don't stop," Asher states.

I glare at him, at his perfect face, then straight into his beautiful blue eyes. He's still an asshole, but I stop pacing and hop up onto the counter with my legs dangling off the edge.

He stalks toward me; I immediately close my legs. He laughs at my feeble attempt, pushes them apart, and steps in between my now open thighs. I resist the urge to wrap my legs around his stomach as if it's something that I would naturally do. Goddamn it. I curse my choice of an outfit again for the night as my dress raises high enough making my red lace thong visible. His eyes glide down then back up to my face with a smirk playing on his lips.

"Need me to distract you, Spade?"

"That's not my name."

"Mmhmm," he mumbles, moving in closer till his mouth is hovering over my jaw. He smells minty, with a trace of whiskey on his breath. His hands are lazily on the side of my thighs, moving up and down trailing his fingers on my bare legs. Sparks shoot straight through my body from his gentle touch. He has killed people before with the same hands that are grazing my skin lightly. The man is a walking contradiction.

"You have to stop," I force out, pushing his hands off my legs. My brain is foggy. I can't think with him this close to me.

"Do I?"

"Yes, I have a boyfriend," I blurt out again, knowing it might stop him. Plus, I do have a boyfriend. I'm not lying to him. He would see anyway if I was. I wouldn't call myself girlfriend of the year from all the lies I've told Blake, but I absolutely will not cheat on him.

Asher's face goes red, his eyes narrowing before changing it back to expressionless. His hands pressed flat against the countertops on each side of me, his muscular arms caging me in. "I told you I don't give a shit about your pig boyfriend." He's in my face seething.

His jaw is locked tight; my body shrinks down on instinct, which seems to make him angrier. I'm about to respond, but I'm saved by the sound of the front door opening. He lets go and backs away as I hop off the counter and run to the door. I feel my heart squeeze as Chase walks in, an absolute bloody mess, but alive.

"Chase! Thank God!" I jump into his arms as he winces, but I don't care. I don't care that my dress is now streaked with blood. My arms are wrapped around him tightly, and I'm so happy that he's okay, a sob escapes my lips. "I was so worried about you."

His body suddenly goes stiff in my arms. I pick up my head from his shoulder to see what's wrong, then I remember who walked in behind me.

"What the hell is he doing here?" Chase screams, the vein in his temple throbbing.

"Chase this is Asher," I reply calmly.

"I know who the fuck he is, but what is this criminal doing here?" Chase's body is shaking with rage as I untangle myself from him.

I close my eyes inhaling a deep breath. Asher is not going to let my brother get away with talking about him like he isn't standing a few feet away. Body heat immediately warms my back. Asher is towering over me from behind now. I'm the only barrier separating the two of them from ripping each other part. The tension in the room is unbelievably thick. I have to defuse the situation. There is no way this night can get any worse.

I turn around and face Asher. His jaw is clenching; his body language is reading murderous. He refuses to look down at me as I try to gain his attention. He's too busy shooting daggers at my brother's eyes over my head.

I put my hand on his chest, feeling his heart racing under my touch. Without thinking, I bring my other hand up to his cheek, palming it lightly trying to calm him down "Please let me stitch him up and talk to him."

Asher takes a step back, to my surprise, but not before giving Chase a long hard stare. "Call me a criminal again I will gladly show you how much of one I can be." He threatens, and I know without a doubt that he would, reminding me again this man is dangerous. Even with his face hard and shooting murderous glares at my brother, I still can't help thinking how hot he looks. *I'm so screwed.*

With his eyes still locked on my brother, sending silent threats, he bends over and places a gentle kiss on my forehead, "Tomorrow night at eight," he reminds me, then walks out the door.

"What the—"

I hold up my hand and cut Chase off before he even begins. He looks like hell. His face grows paler by the second from the blood loss causing me to jump into action. "Sit the hell down. I have to clean you up." I pull out a chair and point to it.

I have had a night from freaking hell and am

through with everyone's macho man complexes. He sits without fuss. I can tell he's in too much pain to fight me, judging by the amount of blood still pouring through his shirt. I run to the bathroom and grab the first aid kit, alcohol (my personal favorite, makes even the manliest men cry like little boys), and a wet towel. His shirt is gone when I return so I can see the extent of the damage. There is a three-inch cut running horizontally along the side of his torso where the knife must have grazed. Most people would squirm at the injury, but this is just another Friday night for me.

"Cut's not deep, you won't need any stitches."

He grunts in response, wincing every time I get near a bruised area of his body. The white towel is red with blood when I finish wiping down all his cuts. Luckily, I don't think most of the blood belonged to him. I figure now is as good of a time as any to replay the night to him while I clean and bandage all the wounds. I tell him about the poker match and how I lost. I explain to him the deal I made, and I can almost feel the anger rolling off him in waves. I quickly change to how he saved me from the fight, pulled me out, and brought me here. My story is finished just as I apply the last butterfly bandage across his eyebrow.

"No." He shakes his head slamming his closed fists down on his legs. "Over my dead body will you go live with him. Only my sister would make a deal with that psycho! You do know he went to jail right?"

"Chase, I got the money, and he has connections I don't doubt Tyler will be out by the morning!" I try to reason.

"I would have found another way!" His voice grows louder. "What the hell could he want with you anyway? None of this makes any sense!"

"Wow, asshole." I know what he wants from me. He wants to make me his sex toy, but how do can I tell my older brother that? Easily I just don't.

"Shit, Kye. I didn't mean it like that; you know you're a beautiful girl." His voice softens when he calls me my childhood name.

"Save it." I hold my hands out defensively. "I did what I had to do for this family. I got Tyler out and that was the plan. I'll be fine. I'm a big girl I can handle myself fine. I'm going to bed. Screw you very much." With a one-finger salute, I walk out and head toward my room and slam the door. Brothers can be such jerks.

Chapter Six

Asher

"Should have walked away," I mumble to no one.

Jimmy raises his eyebrow at me as he casually leans against the limo." One last stop tonight?"

"Yeah," that is all I tell him. That is all I need to say to him. He knows where I need to be without me having to clue him in, and he doesn't question me about it either.

Funny to think I met Jimmy in jail. He was in for armed robbery at only twenty-two. He had already served two of his five-year sentence. He was one of the biggest guys in there and my cellmate. He didn't bother me, and I didn't bother him. That was how our friendship began. It worked for the both of us, and once he got out, he started working for me. He didn't have any family or anywhere to go on the outside, so I recruited him. Best thing to come out of my short time in jail was his loyalty.

Last stop of the night. It's a little after three now which is nothing new for me to be out on the streets this late. The nighttime has ruled my life for the past ten years. I crave the darkness; I thrive in it. After twelve a.m. every night, I'm more alive than I'll ever be. Living every day like me makes sleep more of a bad habit than a necessity. It is also the longest thing a person will ever do in life. Once I'm dead, my body will be in a permanent state of sleep, so why do it now while I'm alive?

The car stops on the east side of the city where anyone can find cheap prostitutes and just about any drug in abundance. I am here for neither. I'm here to clean up the last mess of the shit storm the Turner trio stirred up tonight.

Should have walked away, I think again. I should have left Kylie's piece of shit cop boyfriend to deal with all of this, but I just couldn't do it. Did my need for revenge against him drive me to take all this extra shit on? I don't know, but I refuse to think it was anything else. I know she is not a permanent part in all of this. I can't be feeling shit for her. She will never forgive me in the end, and I don't need any complications in my life.

Then I think of how she looked with her legs wide-open, hanging off the counter. The feel of her thighs hugging my hips while I was standing between them. The tiny, lacy red strip of fabric was covering her pussy that peeked out from under her dress. Fuck. She looked beautiful.

I'm out of the limo looking at the run down house. There is no beauty found here, or at least one would think so at first glance. The shutters are hanging off, and this place looks ready to collapse at any second. The outside is just a front though. Walking through those doors is like being transported into another realm. A realm where girls are dancing around in lingerie and it cost one hundred dollars to get a blowjob. I know this because this is one of the few brothels I own around the city.

I also know he is in here waiting to blow off some

steam from the fight. He comes here after every battle in the Pit, wins or losses. People are creatures of habit. Like I told Kylie earlier tonight, I know my criminals. That was the truth; it is the only way that allows me always to be one step ahead of the game. This asshole screwed up big tonight. He brought a knife into the Pit. The Pit is for men who fight, man-to-man, fist-to-fist. There are a time and place for weapons; the Pit is not the place especially going against an unarmed opponent. It was a real pussy move; one I refuse to take lightly.

"Ash baby," Caitlyn coos, wrapping her arm around me once I'm in the door. "What can I do for you tonight?"

"I'm here for business." I unwrap her body from mine "You see Hunter come in tonight?"

She frowns at me. "Up the stairs first door to the right. He's in there with Kim."

I make my way up the steps. I leave Jimmy behind sitting on a couch talking to one of the girls and tell him to watch the front door. Not even bothering to knock, I throw the door open. Kim is naked and straddling Hunter. Unfazed, she turns her head and looks at me. Her eyes widen when she realizes it's me standing in the door.

"Out," I tell her, and she is up and out of the room faster than a junkie at a drug bust, leaving Hunter and me alone.

He's only wearing his jeans. His ribs are wrapped and taped up, and his face is swollen sporting the aftermath of coming toe to toe with the tank. By looking at him in this condition, I'm not even sure how he planned on fucking anything tonight. Then I see it in his eyes; they are bloodshot with a hint of fear behind them. It's easy to tell a lot about a person just by looking into their eyes. His are telling me that he is high, probably snorted coke and took a bunch of painkillers to numb the pain.

"If this is about the knife, I swear I was going to intimidate him." He throws his hands in the air. He knows very well why I'm here, and he immediately gets defensive trying to feed me some bullshit story.

This isn't my first rodeo. Next will come the pleading and begging me to spare his pathetic life. Followed by the promise that he will do anything I ask of him. The last part always brings me back to being a kid when I believed in a god and would promise him I would go to church every Sunday if he granted my wish. How many times do you think I went to church after that?

"Bringing the knife to the Pit was your first mistake. Your second was threatening what is mine." I strike without any warning; my hand wraps around his throat.

He's trying to fight me off, but between the adrenaline crash from the fight and the number of drugs, his senses are delayed. His arms are flailing, and he's clawing at my shirt. He's no match for me in the state he is currently in. It takes about three minutes for the brain to become damaged due to loss of oxygen. At about ten minutes, the change of recovery is unlikely, and about fifteen before Hunter's body is slumped onto the ground dead. I pick up my burner and call my guy to come clean up the room and leave no traces of me being here behind. I'll have one of the girls call it in later. It would be like I was never even here. To my advantage, there are drugs in his system. This could quickly be ruled as an overdose.

"Chris, I need a cleanup." I rattle off the address to him, but before I hang up, I tell him, "If you see something you like downstairs, come back here when the jobs are done and tell her it's on me." I always take care of my own.

I take one last look at the man on the floor. I didn't have to kill him. Under different circumstances, I would have roughed him up a bit and forbid him from fighting in the Pit again. That wouldn't have been enough to satisfy the beast within me, though. He's been stirring since I watched Hunter lock eyes on Kylie and give her a warning grin. That was all it took for me to decide he was a dead man. My little firecracker surprised me when she took a step to go after him. She couldn't have been standing taller than five foot six, even with those heels on, but she was ready to take him on. There isn't anything she wouldn't do for her brothers; she proved that when she made a deal with me. I admire the loyalty she has for her family, and that is a problem because there is no room in my life to respect anyone, especially not the enemy's girl.

Jimmy is waiting for me downstairs with a shit-eating grin on his face. Only one thing could give him that look. "I told you to watch the door, asshole. We were here on business."

"I did watch the door." He throws his hand up pointing. "See that room across from us. I kept it cracked open the whole time."

"Oh yeah? And what were you planning to do with your nightstick and grenades hanging out?"

His jaw drops leaving his mouth hanging open,

"Did you refer to my dick and balls as a nightstick and grenades?"

I shake my head trying to hold in the laugh attempting to break out. "I was trying to prove a point. Your dick and balls are hardly a weapon of defense."

"True, but they have slain a ton of pussy," he says back grinning.

This time I'm unable to hold back my laughter.

Chapter Seven

Kylie

I wake up to a hand lightly caressing my face. I look up at him. His green eyes are tired, and he's still in uniform, so he must have just gotten off work. In the beginning, I loved how he looked in his uniform, and now I find myself thinking about the man on the other side of the law.

"Good morning, baby," he says.

"Morning, Blake." I lean up and give him a sweet kiss on the lips. He tastes like coffee, which he most likely lived on through the night to stay awake.

We've been dating for about a year now, but we've never had the serious talk. He has tried a few times, and every time, I've managed to throw a different excuse at him as to why I won't let him fully in my life.

The truth is my family and I haven't exactly been model citizens. I know I will never be able to tell him half the shit that goes on in my life. I can never allow him to get too close, so I keep him at arm's length to put it best.

The lies I tell him continuously weigh pretty heavy on my conscience. I'm not a heartless person. I know he doesn't deserve it, but what else am I supposed to do? He's a freaking cop. One who could lose the job that he loves if I drag him into my world. Sure, he knows about my brothers; he would need to live under a rock not to hear about half the activities they do. Somehow, he thinks I've managed to stay innocent through all of it. Proving the theory how love is blind.

He lays down next to me in bed and wraps his hard body around mine. My mind drifts off to the feel of Asher's strong arms wrapped around me, making me feel safe. Quickly, I shove that thought to the back of my mind and fall back into the comfort of Blake's body.

I do love the feel of him. He is a great guy, and my heart breaks a little because I know what has to be done today. The guilt begins to seep inside of me. Breaking it off is going to crush him, but there is no way I can live with and sleep with another man, while still dating him.

The deal was in place; there is nothing I can do now. It has to be upheld. My family will always come first. They are everything to me. I have no idea what would have happened to me if I didn't have them to lean on all those years.

I turn my body around so that Blake and I are lying face to face. I run the tips of my fingers down his jaw and over his lips. He is a complete pretty boy with his blond curly hair that falls over his forehead, and his dark green eyes.

He studies my mouth before leaning over and capturing my lips with his. His kiss is sweet and loving; it feels nice. He pulls away and starts moving down my jaw and neck, leaving a trail of light kisses on the way.

My eyes closed, and all I can see is Asher's face. I try to force the image away and get lost in Blake, but I can't. "Blake, stop," I force out. I can't do this to him.

"What's wrong, baby?" He lays a kiss on my forehead then my nose. All I can think about now is how much I'm about to hurt him.

"We need to talk." I push the words out trying not to think about what I'm about to do. The four words that no one in any relationship ever wants to hear. Those four words have the power to destroy someone like I am about to do now.

"Okay." His brows scrunch together. "What's going on?"

He's so damn sweet it pains me. I start to debate the "it's not you, it's me" but then stop myself before it comes out. But it is me. I promised to sleep another man. He deserves better than an excuse though.

He deserves better than me. He should be with someone who doesn't hide half her life from him. "I can't do this with you anymore. I'm sorry. You deserve better than what I'm giving you."

"You can't do this anymore?" he repeats my words back to me with a pained look on his face.

"Yeah." That's all I say. There isn't anything else to say. I can't even bear looking at him. My heart is hurting just from the thought of what he must be feeling.

"Okay, if that is what you want. Take your time and remember that I love you, Kye." He looks at me with so much sadness and says nothing else. He gets up from my bed and starts picking up his discarded uniform from the floor and puts it on.

I wish he would say something and stop being so nice about it, tell me I'm wrong! Question my reasoning! Fight for me! Anything! But he doesn't, and he won't because he carries around guilt from a past relationship. One that if I ever tried to bring up, he would shut me down right away. The only thing he would tell me was that he ended up hurting people he loved and that she passed away.

My heart broke for him the day he told me. With tears in his eyes and the pain he felt evident on his face. I never brought her up again.

He walks out my door without glancing back. He doesn't have it in himself to make me feel bad. He was always too good for me, and deep down I've known it. Once I hear the front door shut, I force myself to roll out of bed. I have no time to lie in bed all day and dwell on the fact that a piece of my heart went out the door with him.

After a shower and a change of clothes, I make my way into our tiny kitchen. We've updated it the best we could through the years, but everything is still old and outdated. The original wood cabinets are still hanging over the counters. Last year we finally replaced the tops with granite because the Formica wasn't holding up well. The walls are covered in wallpaper with chickens plastered on it; they used to scare me when I was younger, which is why I think Chase and Tyler won't let me tear it down. Then in the center of the room is a small kitchen table where Chase is sitting, eating leftover pizza for breakfast.

"That is disgusting," I tell him making a face. "It's only ten a.m."

He lifts the glass of milk he's drinking and shakes it back and forth. "Duh, that's why I have milk."

I roll my eyes then make myself a bowl of cereal before taking the seat across from him. It's weird sitting at the table without Tyler. I miss having both pains in the ass here in the morning shoving the previous night's conquest out the door.

45

"How did that go?" He nods his head toward the door, and I'm guessing he means with Blake.

I sigh. "I told him I couldn't see him anymore."

He studies my face looking for a trace of something, but I won't give him what he is looking for. Saying he was never on board with me dating a cop is an understatement. For months, I've tried convincing him that it was nothing serious between us, but I don't think he ever really believed me. I don't blame him because a part of me will always love Blake, but I don't think I was ever in love with him.

"For what it is worth, I think you did the right thing letting him go."

Yup. I knew that was coming. I let a good honest man walk out the door, and my brother thinks I did the right thing. Typical. "Hear anything from Tye, yet?" I change the subject.

"Yeah, he called an hour ago. He's out just like you said he would be," he replies. "He had to stop at the shop." By shop, he means chop shop. "I think he had a few things he needed to clean up." And by that, he means he had to get all the illegal stuff out before the cops come in and search the place again.

"Okay. Well I need to pack my bags for my trip to hell. I have a date with Hades later," I joke trying to make light of the situation.

"Kylie, it's not a joke." He slams his hands on the table. "Asher Black is a dangerous criminal!"

"And what exactly are you, asshole? We sure aren't nice church going people last time I checked." My blood boils. Here we are fighting again. Shows how much we need Tye home. He was always the levelheaded one out of us three.

Without another word, he gets up and storms out of the kitchen. That's the second man I love that I've chased away today, and it's only ten a.m. A new personal record for me.

Chapter Eight

Kylie

Eight o'clock on the dot, I'm standing outside my house with four full packed suitcases. I have no idea how long I will be staying, and a girl needs her things. Wiping the nervous sweat from my brow even though it's a chilly Chicago night, I wonder what Asher has in store for me. Before I can change my mind, a black truck pulls up and stops on the street in front of me, taking away my last chance to escape. Even his ride screams murder with tinted windows and all black rims. I shouldn't have expected anything less.

He said he would be sending a driver, but even through the dark glass windows, I know it is him in the driver's seat. There isn't anyone living on this block who would be driving a new truck. Well, not now since Tyler had been arrested, that is.

Asher steps out of the truck and walks over to me. He's wearing a black button up tonight, both sleeves folded up to just above his elbows with a pair of jeans that mold perfectly to his legs. Asher Black is any girls walking fantasy, and with the grin he just shot me, he knows precisely the effect he has on the opposite sex.

"Keep looking at me like that, darlin', and I'll start to think you're happy about this arrangement."

"I just wasn't expecting you to pick me up. That's all," I say, feeling my cheeks blush.

He gives me a cocky smile and bends down, placing a small peck on my cheek. My breathing hitches. *Good grief, Kylie, it was only a kiss on the cheek.* Gathering up my bags in his hands, he heads back to his truck and gestures me to follow. Lowering the tailgate of his pick-up, he loads my bags in.

"I guess you dumped the body before picking me up then," I tease nervously.

Asher gives me a humorless smile. "Get in."

I'd rather not, but I do it anyway. "I'll remember not to joke with you again," I mumble, hopping into the passenger seat.

We drive through the city until we reach its limits. The tall buildings and city lights pass behind us leaving them in the rearview mirror, as we continue through rural parts now.

Inside the truck, the ride has been entirely silent. A nervous feeling takes over my body, leaving me curious as to why we would be driving away from the city. The seriousness of the situation finally hits me. I barely even know this man, and from the stories I've heard, I don't want to know him. My body breaks out in a nervous sweat. Rubbing my palms against my thighs, I take in deep breaths to calm myself.

I cling to the positive thought that I've been alone with him a few times already, and I have a feeling if a man like Asher wants you dead, he isn't going to waste any time. Maybe that isn't such a positive thought, but there's truth to it. Oddly enough, I haven't felt myself in danger around him. On the contrary, I've felt safe with him, which is even more dangerous, for my heart at least.

"Where are we going?" I finally gain the courage

to ask, steadying my words. He is, after all, the most dangerous criminal I've heard of, and that says something when you live among them.

"To my house, relax." He pauses as if he could hear the thoughts running through my head, "And for the record, I don't keep the bodies in my trunk, leaves behind too much evidence." He looks over at me, flashing his panty-dropping smile.

I'm not confident if he is joking or not. I let out a small nervous laugh. I have yet to see a playful side to him, so he's probably serious. Although, I don't think he wants to add me to his hidden pile of dead bodies. I haven't given him any reason for it. Plus, he saved me from the fights in the Pit, right? Why would he take me so that he could kill me? Then I wonder why this man does anything that he does.

"So, can you tell me something about yourself?" I ask, after a few minutes of silence.

"No," his reply is clipped. I glare at him before he abruptly pulls over onto a dead-end street. "Get out," he says once the car comes to a stop.

"No, I'm good here." I shake my head staring at my hands folded across my lap.

Reaching his body over mine, he pulls my door handle open. "Kylie, get out."

This time I listen. Only a minute later he joins me outside the car with a stern look on his handsome face. "I don't think this is necessary." Standing up to my full height of five foot four, I can hear Chase's words raddling my brain; *never show fear.* He isn't much of a poet, but I find myself repeating the phrase in my head till I'm standing even taller.

"Want to know what I think?" Asher's arms fold

across his chest.

"No, not really," I reply, instantly regretting it.

Asher storms toward me, his legs making the long powerful stride. He doesn't stop till he has me trapped between the car and his body. I feel every inch of him pressed up against the length of me. The metal from the vehicle digs into my back as his solid abs press into my front. Fear mixed with anger courses through me, but my skin buzzes with electricity from his closeness.

I can feel his breath against my ear, leaning in closer he talks into it calmly, "I think we had a deal. I think asking questions and getting to know me wasn't part of it. There is nothing I can tell you about myself that you want to hear. I suggest you stop asking questions that deep down you don't want the answers to." Once he stops talking, I feel him press a trail of light kisses from my ear down to my collarbone.

My heart begins racing, and he's pushed so tightly against me there's no way for me to hide how my body reacts to him. His lips smile against my skin.

I'm paralyzed in my spot, afraid if he backs away I'll fall to the ground into a pile of mush. He picks his head back up, and his void blue eyes meet mine. I look away embarrassed.

"Look at me," he demands.

I shake my head and keep my eyes down. I don't want him to see the redness in my cheeks and the lust in my eyes. I can't let him know that he's gotten to me.

"Kylie, pick your head up and look at me." I begin to shake my head again before his hand wraps around my jaw, forcing my face up meet his. "Now nod your head that you agree with what we are doing here." I don't even get the chance to. He uses the hand wrapped around my jaw nodding my head for me.

"Good girl." He presses his lips to mine for a quick kiss. "Now get back in." Then he's gone, backed away from me, and getting into the car as if nothing just happened.

I take a few minutes to recover, needing time to get my mind and body to function as one. Eventually, I'm able to stand up straight and get back in. Great job at showing him how unaffected you are, ho.

The rest of the ride is silent as we keep driving for another ten minutes before he turns onto a beautiful, clean, quiet street on the outskirts of the city. Kids are playing soccer outside, using garbage cans as goal post barriers. They are having a ball laughing and running around. When we approach, they scatter to the sides; even children are smart enough to back away from him. The moms that were standing around talking stop their conversations and stare. Most likely they are aware of who he is.

I find myself wondering if it's always like this for him. People always look at him with fear in their eyes as if he's about to go on a murdering spree, even when he's doing something as mundane as driving.

I look over at him and catch him watching me. I give him a weak smile. I don't know why I did it, but for a minute, I felt sorry for him. He clears his throat, turning his attention back to the road and continues driving to the end. Finally, he pulls off onto a long driveway and throws his truck into park.

The driveway leads up to an old, beautiful, two-story Victorian house with a wraparound porch. The house is set back enough that it leaves a ton of open land around the front and in the back. I look over at him to find him staring at me.

"That is your house?" My mouth hangs open.

His eyes narrow at me in anger. His hands grip the steering wheel turning his knuckles white before he releases it. He throws the car door open and gets out, leaving the slamming door in his wake.

I wasn't expecting that quick change of attitude from him, even though I just treated him the same way everyone else does. Feeling guilty, I get out of the car and follow him up the steps.

"I'm sorry," I apologize. "I didn't mean anything by it."

"It's just a house, Kylie, a place to sleep nothing more nothing less." His tone is clipped as he grabs my bags from the back and heads toward the door.

I follow thinking about his response. For a minute, I could almost feel the loneliness from his tone. Maybe I've judged him completely wrong. He hasn't done anything to make me genuinely feel like I'm in danger, although I already contemplated in my head the thousand different ways he could end me.

"It's beautiful." I find myself confessing once we walk in the door. His home is beautiful, and that's what it exactly is, a home. The walls are all painted warm colors around the open concept floor plan. His living room has a large pit leather couch that I could see myself curling up on watching movies. His kitchen also has all new granite counters with stainless steel appliances. Through the window, I can see his backyard has a deck with a fire pit off to the side.

All through the house has a homey vibe, the lack of photos tugs at my heart leaving me wondering if he has any family. There is a soft woman's touch here, and that makes me think at one time if this was the house he shared with his deceased wife.

He was married once years ago. I was sixteen at the time, and I can remember it like it was recently. The story was on the news for weeks about the notorious Asher Black's wife being killed by a drunk driver a month after he was released from prison. She was pregnant at the time. That day he lost both his wife and his baby. My heart breaks a little for him as I catch him staring at me. I wonder if that is the reason he is cold and distant now.

"Come on. I will show you our room." He grabs my hand to lead me up the stairs.

I pull my hand away when I let the words "our room" sink in, as if we were an actual couple. "Um, I don't think so. You can show me to the guest room."

He turns around reaching out his hand, grabbing a strand of my hair and pushing it behind my ear. I try to swat his hand away. He catches my wrist in the air wrapping his fingers tightly around. "We had a deal, Miss Turner. You agreed to stay in my bed, so you will. If you want to go back on the deal, I'm sure I can let the cops know where Tyler keeps the rest of the cars."

My mouth drops in shock. I underestimated how cruel he can be. To think for a second, I began to feel sorry for him. Letting my guard down is not a mistake to make again.

His grip gets tighter around my wrist when I try to pull away again. This time I don't say anything and allow him to drag me up the old wooden stairs. There is no point trying to argue. He's right this is what I signed up for, to play house with a felon, and nothing will make me risk Tyler being sent back to jail. Even if I have to deal with his mood swings.

He lets go when we reach the master bedroom, and it is enormous, probably larger than my entire house. I can tell he picked out the furniture in here with the sleek back dresser and bed frame. The comforter is black and gray. The whole room screams masculinity. There's a large flat screen TV on the wall across from the king size bed.

I walk into the connecting bathroom, and it is gorgeous. The walk-in shower has three different heads, and one is a waterfall. There's also a gigantic tub on the other side of the bathroom as well. I'm in complete awe of his entire house.

"He doesn't deserve such a beautiful house." I jump at the sound of him clearing his throat, not realizing he followed me in here.

I turn to face him, and his blue eyes pull me in immediately. I hate how captivating his eyes are, and it's like they can see right through me. His presence leaves my mind in a jumble. I can't think straight around him when he looks at me like this. He is painfully gorgeous, but he is also not a good person and a criminal, I remind myself.

He walks closer to me, reaching for the wrist he dragged me upstairs with. Once in his grasp, he lightly strokes his thumb around it. He brings my wrist up to his lips, placing a feathery kiss on the inside.

I stop breathing with him so close to me; he catches my reaction, let's go, and then steps away from me.

"Unpack your bags, take a shower, and get settled. I have somewhere to be. Don't wait up for me." His voice turns cold so fast as he turns around and walks out the door. His mood swings have me in a whirlwind that's impossible to keep up with.

Just like that, I'm left entirely alone in Asher Black's house. I shiver at the thought.

Chapter Nine

Asher

I needed to get out fast before she said something to piss me off again. I lied to her telling I had somewhere to be. Technically, I do have somewhere to be, and right now, it is where ever the hell she isn't.

Having her there in the house I shared with Angelina brought back memories. Ones that I thought I had buried with her long ago, which is what triggered my pissed off attitude, to begin with.

I haven't felt the loss of my wife in a long time, but watching Kylie look around the house brought me back to the first day Angelina stepped inside the very same house. Kylie's face mirrored her expression, both in complete awe.

Those were different times, and I was a different man back then. I was young, in love, and stupid, and I had plenty of money, looking back now I think of how much of a dangerous combo that was. All I wanted to do then was please her, and in the end, it all blew the fuck up in my face. Now I have Kylie getting under my skin. I won't allow myself to let my guard down with her. I'm not that man anymore; I remind myself. I'm not even a decent man now. I push back all the old memories and head back to the city.

Once I make it back in the VIP room above my club, I pour myself some whiskey. Swirling it around the glass, I wonder if this was a horrible decision. Am I in as much control as I like to believe I am? Taking a swig back, I feel the burn before pouring myself another glass. I need to clear my head before I can return to the house, back to Kylie and her big innocent green eyes.

I rest my elbow on my knees. Shaking my head. I really shouldn't have grabbed her wrist like that. Fuck, acting the way I just did around her will get me nowhere. I need her to trust me. I need her to believe the stories about me aren't true. Once I can touch her without her flinching, I know I won't be able to stop myself from taking what I want, but I need her to want it too.

The most screwed up part is my physical attraction to her. I wanted nothing more than to throw her against the wall and go down on her after she threw her little sassy attitude at me. I need to hear my name fall from her lips over and over while she comes in my mouth. That would be the best revenge against officer asshole that I could ask for, as well as the hottest thing in the world. I'm not even sure what I want more, at this point.

The problem is Kylie won't give in to me quickly. She's going to be some work. I need to make her fall for me. I need to earn her trust, and so far, she's been taking things pretty well. She's strong deep down; she had to be when growing up. Her only parents were two teenage thug boys. I hope she's strong enough to come out of this still intact.

A knock on the door pulls me from the inner war going on in my head. "Come in."

A second later Jimmy walks in. "Someone is here

to see you," he tells me. "It's Kylie's brother."

God no. I'm not in the mood to deal with that loose cannon. "Tell Chase I said for him to fuck off."

"No, not Chase. It's Tyler."

I sigh. "All right bring him up." I hope he is nothing like his brother or even his sister for that matter; she has a fiery little temper too.

Jimmy walks in with Tyler and closes the door. Tyler takes a seat across from me while Jimmy stands tall behind him. He does this every time we have a visitor. Always ready to take down anyone who steps out of line.

Tyler sits there looking at ease. His shoulders are relaxed and his legs are crossed at his ankles. Complete different demeanor than his brother and sister. All three-look similar though, with the same blond hair and facial structure. From body language alone, I'm able to tell he is different from the other two. A few seconds with him in my office, I can see he is calmer and less confrontational. For someone who just got out of prison, he looks like he doesn't have a care in the world.

"Tyler," I address him. "What brings you here?"

"Officer Owens told me you bailed me out, and I wanted to thank you." I watch him looking for any trace of dishonesty, but nothing comes.

"You're thanking me even though I have your little sister in my house as we speak?" I question him, so he understands I'm in control. In case this is a game he's playing, he needs to know he won't win.

"Yeah," he pauses. "I have my concerns about why you have her. She's my younger sister, but I also know she hasn't done anything to you for her life to be in danger. Am I correct?"

I can already tell I like him. He's much smarter than his hotheaded brother. Hard to believe this man is his twin. I could use a levelheaded man like Tyler to work for me, but I think his sister would have my nuts if I offered. Shit, what is wrong with me? I'm not scared of that little girl.

"My intentions with your sister will not put her in any harm." Physically anyway, but I don't say that out loud. I never have and will never hurt a woman or a child. No matter what, those are my two ground rules. Anyone else is fair game.

"Then we shouldn't have any problems." He narrows his eyes at me enough for me to understand the threat behind his words.

I stand up ready to see him out of my office. "Nope, no problems."

He extends his arm to shake my hand with a firm shake. "Take care of her, Black." He tells me before he's out the door with Jimmy at his heel.

That family is going to be my downfall. I shake my head and refill my glass. I continue to swirl the liquid around in the glass. I find it a habit of mine when I feel control slipping. Those moments are few and far between, yet here I am.

"Sir," I hear Jimmy call out.

"What now?" I rub my hands over my face.

He comes back into the room and switches on the television, "Just thought you might want to see this."

The screen flashes images of the man that was Hunter Lloyd. I feel nothing, not even a hint of remorse as the dead man's picture stares back at me from the screen. The news reporter is standing outside of the Pit stating it as the last place he was seen. The screen changes to a picture of his brother who is claiming to have reason to believe he has gone missing. Of course, he has reason to believe that. He pulled a knife on a fighter. Anyone with half a brain knows if you draw a knife on someone in this neighborhood and don't get the job done, it's going to end in a body bag for you.

I take the last swig of my whiskey. My throat is numb from it. At this point, it's going down like water.

"You think she's watching this?" Jimmy asks.

"I have no idea," I tell him, honestly. I ran out of the house before she had time to do much of anything, "But she's not stupid. She's going to know I had something to do with it."

A little after four a.m., I'm quietly opening the door to my house. I close it behind me and stand still listening for any signs of movement from upstairs. When I hear nothing, I make my way up the steps into the bedroom. Relief fills me when I see her passed out on top of the covers wearing a long sleep shirt. The shirt has risen high enough for the bottoms of her perfectly shaped ass cheeks to hang out. I fight myself from reaching out and running my fingers around the curve between the bottom of her ass and top of her thigh. Her body is beautiful, and I am totally screwed for bringing her here.

I strip down in the bathroom and step into the shower. My thoughts keep drifting back to Kylie spread out on my bed in her nightshirt. I place a hand on my already hard cock and pump once. I let my head fall back and close my eyes thinking of her pink lips wrapped around the tip. I pump harder picturing her completely naked on her knees in front of me taking my whole cock in her mouth. I'm almost ready to blow my load when I hear a small gasp. I open my eyes and lock them on her emerald, shocked ones, on the other side of the glass door. Through the steamed glass from the shower, I can see her mouth is open to a perfect O. I don't stop stroking my cock, and she doesn't look away. Her eyes are glued to palm wrapped around my hard dick. I pump a few more times before I come. Her face is a bright shade of pink.

"Enjoy the show?" I ask her with a cocky smile.

"I-I'm sorry." She snaps out of her daze and stutters, turning around she bolts out the door.

Maybe her being here isn't going to be so horrible, I think as I smile toward her retreating frame.

Chapter Ten

Kylie

I wake in the morning to a heavy arm lying across my waist. I look over to a still sleeping Asher on his stomach facing my way. I thought while sleeping a man is supposed to look innocent and boyish. There is nothing innocent or youthful about the man next to me in his sleeping form. His lips are pressed into a straight line, and he has a five o'clock shadow dusting his jaw. His dark brown hair is still perfectly styled. What the heck. He stays beautiful and intimidating even in his sleep. I'm not confident this man is human.

I slowly lift his massive arm off me and slip out of bed. I watch and see his chest rise and fall; he's still sleeping. I make my way into the kitchen to make breakfast. I'm not ready to face him yet. I still can't believe he caught me watching him jerking off just a few hours ago. When I woke up to take a quick pee, I was still half-asleep. I wasn't even aware he came home. Half the time his moves are silent, like the thief that he is.

I rub my hand down my face thinking how I stopped in the middle of the bathroom stunned, like a teenage girl seeing a naked man for the first time. I have seen naked men before, but none like the naked god in the shower in front of me. His body looked like it was sculpted and chiseled out of stone. He had the V that makes grown women do crazy things, underneath a perfectly defined six-pack.

I couldn't look away as he continued to pump his huge dick. It was the most erotic, yet beautiful thing I have ever seen. When he came, I could feel myself soaking wet. I had to close my thighs fast to calm my throbbing core. His eyes never strayed from mine. Not once did he look embarrassed about being caught pleasuring himself. Instead, he looked like he enjoyed himself while his hand jerked his cock in front of me. I think it turned him on even more.

Blake would have died in embarrassment if I walked in on him doing that. He lacked the adventurous side in the bedroom. Sex with Blake was gentle and passionate; we made love. I'm confident with Asher it would be nothing but hard, fast, and rough.

Physically, Blake's body is the closest one I have seen that would hold up against Asher's. They both stood around the same height and weight, but Asher was more rock-solid muscle. Blake also didn't have any ink where Asher had the whole side of his upper body covered in black and gray shaded designs. Neither one lacked in the looks department. I would describe Blake as your boy next door and Asher as your nightmare across the street.

My stomach grumbling has me searching through his cabinets and fridge to see what I can make. I find eggs, bacon, and toast. I turn on the TV that hangs on the brick kitchen wall. The pan I'm holding falls out of my hand landing with a loud thump on the floor, as I stare at the screen in shock.

Asher comes running in with a gun in his hand and looks at me. "What's wrong?" He sets the safety lock back on when he sees there is no immediate danger; he places the gun on the counter.

Staring at me curiously, he follows my line of vision to the television flashing Hunter's pictures. "Shit," he whispers, confirming my thoughts that he had something to do with the man's disappearance.

"Do you have anything to do with this?" I ask in a shaky breath, hoping he tells me, no, but part of me is also hoping he tells me yes, so I know he isn't lying to me.

He does neither; instead, he stays still and silent. "Asher?" I call out to get his attention toward me. When he looks back at me, I raise my eyebrow questioning him silently again.

He goes to open his mouth then closes it. Without a word, he turns around and walks out of the kitchen.

I'm not even upset the man is dead. He deserved what he had coming to him. I'm not sure how I feel about Asher taking a life. I'm not stupid enough to believe this is the first or last time for him but never have I been tied to murder before or one that has affected me directly. What if the cops trace this back to Chase or me? But if I know anything, it is that Asher Black left zero traces behind. If that idea is supposed to make me feel any better, it does the exact opposite. I should have never agreed to come here.

I finish making breakfast in a daze when Asher makes his way back into the kitchen dressed for the day. He comes over and places food on his plate. I make mine and sit across from him at the table. A surreal feeling hits me; we're like your average couple eating together in the morning before work.

He makes a few attempts at small talk, but I only

nod my head or shake it back and forth in response. Once we finish, I grab his plate and mine then head to the sink to wash them. Asher walks up behind me; he stops behind me pressing his front into my back. I do my best at ignoring him as I focus on scrubbing an already clean plate.

He bends his head down till I can feel his lips press lightly behind my ear. Ignoring him is becoming increasingly impossible the longer I feel him pressed against me. I scrub the dish harder as a distraction till soap is splattering everywhere. His body vibrates behind me with laughter. His one hand wraps around my front and stops at the base of my neck, rubbing the pads of his fingers lightly against my flesh.

"Your pulse is racing." He tells me as if I don't already know that. "You can be pissed at me all you want for killing that piece of shit, but I don't regret it." With that, he pulls my jaw back enough till he's able to place a sweet kiss on my lips. "I will kill for what's mine."

I take a sharp breath in. "For me? Or because I belong to you?" I ask, already knowing the answer. He killed Hunter because he considers me his possession, and if he hadn't gone after the man who threatened me, people would see him as weak. As twisted as it is, I still hoped that it was to protect me, but I'm smarter than believing that.

He smiles against my lips, kissing them again before he walks out the door, leaving my question hanging in the air.

If I know one thing, it's that if every morning is like this, we are going to have the cleanest dishes ever.

****

A week passes by where we have gotten into a comfortable, silent routine. I wake up in the morning and make us breakfast. We eat in complete silence then his driver takes me to work. After work, I come back here and cook dinner. Asher never makes it home in time to eat, so I leave his plate wrapped on the stove and have dinner with a glass of wine and a book by myself. Then I usually check in with Chase or Tyler through a burner phone that Asher leaves me in the morning. The only three numbers ever programmed in the phones are his and my two brother's.

The day after the news blew up about a missing Hunter, I was due to return to teaching. That was the first and last chat we've had all week.

"I'll have a driver take you to school," he told me, knowing that I return to work today.

"That is unnecessary. Hand me over one of the keys to one of your sports cars in the garage," I replied, being completely serious.

He lets out the first honest laugh I've heard from him. "Over my dead body." I thought he was beautiful enough just standing there, but when he laughs he is hands-down startling.

Still, I rolled my eyes at him because I was pissed off. Men and their cars. "Fine jerk, tell him to pick me up at three-thirty."

Fighting with him about it was pointless. All though he does let me come and go as I please, it doesn't feel like complete freedom with always having a driver lurking around. I'm sure Asher puts them up to it. He still needs to control the situation by knowing where I am and who I'm with at all times. He also needs to make sure that I'm not going to run on him.

The thought of running hasn't even crossed my mind since the day I lost my complete freedom in the poker game. I'm not one to go back on my word. I do wonder why he has yet to claim me by screwing me like he promised. I thought that was the whole reason he brought me here in the first place. I guess I can't act like I have been approachable all week. I was still pissed about the whole Hunter thing, plus I had PMS, so I can't be held responsible for my attitude.

The hardest part is having him sleep close to me. I wait for him to touch me, and he doesn't. I'm not even sure why I crave his touch at all. Well yes, I do. I haven't been able to get the image of him in the shower out of my head. As much as I want to fight him off for coming close to me, I also want to pull him in and feel his lips on mine. The feeling is contradicting. My mind tells me to stay far away from him, but my body craves him. He's too enticing for his good. He's like my version of the forbidden fruit.

I fix myself a glass of red wine and head to the bedroom with a romance novel in hand. I make myself comfortable in his king size bed and take in a deep breath. My nose is instantly assaulted with the smell of his cologne, and oddly enough, it relaxes me. I feel safe in his home and his bed.

After a few more glasses, I put the book down on the nightstand next to me. I lay in the dark thinking about Asher's tempting body while I toss and turn. I don't know how much longer I can go on sleeping next to him without having him touch me.

Needing some relief, I slowly start to pick up the sides of my nightshirt leaving my bottom half-bare. I'm conflicted, knowing how bad it is for me to do this while I'm in Asher's bed with him not here. I'm getting even wetter at the thought of It. Knowing how wrong it would be to pleasure myself here is an instant turn on. I lie back on his bed and close my eyes while I run my hand up the inside of my thigh lightly. I grab my one nipple through my shirt with my other hand and pinch it slightly. A small moan leaves my lips when I trail a finger through my parted lips. I'm lost to the world when the instant I find my clit I started rubbing it on small circles. My breathing increases I'm unaware of the bed dipping next to me.

Chapter Eleven

Asher

What the hell? I think in my head as I hear a moan coming from my bedroom. I came home early tonight after there was a fight at the club. I kicked everyone the hell out. I've been on edge lately. I know it because Kylie has been ignoring me all week.

My steps become angrier the closer I get to my room. Her heavy breathing and moans are loud enough to wake the fucking dead. If she is in there with someone, I will kill him and her. I stop dead in my tracks once I walk through my bedroom doorway. I'm stunned at the sight before my eyes. Kylie is lying on my bed with her shirt only covering the top half of her body and her bottom half completely naked and bare. I can see her wet pussy from where I'm standing through her parted thighs. She's working her little fingers around her clit, and it's the hottest thing I've ever seen in my life.

I make my way closer to the bed as her breathing hitches. She's still unaware I'm here. I place one hand on the bed next to her gently till her eyes finally pop open to me leaning over her.

She completely stills before she tries to pull her shirt down to cover her body. Her expression mirrors a kid with her hand caught in the cookie jar. I stop her by grabbing both of her wrists and hold them together above her head.

"Don't cover up on my behalf darlin'. That was fucking sexy." My voice is deep and strained. I'm fighting control as I feel my hard cock rubbing against my jeans.

Her eyes are clouded, her cheeks a deep shade of red. I use one hand to hold both of hers above her against the bed, as I run my other hand softly down her neck, brushing down the middle of her breasts and stopping on her flat abdomen. She whimpers at my touch and wiggles her body.

"What do you want?" I bring my hand even lower stopping just above her dripping wet pussy. I need her to say it before I touch her there.

"Please," she whispers.

"Please what, Kylie? Do you want my fingers? Tell me," I ask her, holding onto the tiny amount of control I have left.

"Yes," she says, and I barely hear her, but it's enough for me to run a single finger through her slit. She trembles at my touch. Shit, she is soaked.

"Ride my fingers." I push two inside her roughly. Her hips begin to move as her pussy hugs my fingers tightly. I let her hands go so I can use my free one and reach up and pull the shirt off her. I need to see her tits. I have imagined what they looked like since she walked into my club.

Once they are spilling out of her shirt, they are better than I pictured. I bend over her and take her tiny pink nipple in my mouth. I lick slowly then suck hard and take a nip into her flesh causing her to whither below me.

"Oh God," she hisses as I curl my fingers up

against the right spot inside her and rub. She's thrashing her hips wildly against my fingers like it's the last orgasm she's ever going to get.

I change pace to bring them in and out slowly tormenting her. "Want to come for me, baby?"

"Yes, Asher, yes please," she says through moans.

"Okay, baby." I push my fingers in and out faster, then use my thumb to find her clit. That's all it takes for her to scream my name as an orgasm rips through her tight little body. I pull my hand away, bringing my fingers up to my mouth, taking her sweet taste in.

She looks away from my eyes, then down to the boner I'm rocking visibly through my jeans, and she's embarrassed. She's cute to act this way after she rode my fingers begging for release. She starts to grab my pants, and I push her hand away.

"What about you?" she asks me, which is pretty much the longest sentence she's said to me all week. I should pull out my cock and at least let her suck me till I get off, but I back away instead.

"Tonight was about you," I tell her.

She looks up at me with rejection in her eyes from being turned down.

I grab her hand and put it over my jean-clad hard dick, so she feels what she does to me. "Trust me I want you, Kylie. It's killing me not to put my cock in you right now, but I needed to do this for you." I need to do this for you only, so I can earn your trust just to screw you over in the end, I think silently.

"Okay," she whimpers then drops it. "Why are you home early? I wasn't expecting you."

"I think I showed up at the perfect time," I tell her smiling, and she pushes me away from her.

"Don't be a jackass," she says, fighting off a smile.

"It's nice to hear your voice again," I tell her, honestly. "If I knew getting you off would bring you back, I would have done it sooner."

"Just when I thought you were about to say something sweet, you go ahead and ruin it." She picks up a pillow and looks ready to launch it at my face.

"I wouldn't do that if I were—" The pillow hits me in my face cutting my words off. I stand there shocked.

She knows who I am and what I am capable of, and yet she's sitting up on my bed hysterically laughing now. She looks young and carefree as I try to hold back a smile. When did I become such a pussy? If I had to take a guess, it was the moment I felt her tight cunt squeezing against my fingers.

Chapter Twelve

Kylie

After I throw the pillow at Asher and am unable to control my laughter, I immediately regret it. I back away frightened of how he is going to react. He looked shocked as hell that I hit him in the face. I must not have been thinking straight after coming down from an intense orgasm.

He stalks over to me and pushes my body back to lay flat on the bed. He crawls on top of me with his legs straddling my hips. His hands go underneath my sleep shirt that I put back on, up to the side of my bare stomach and he starts tickling my skin.

"Ah, stop stooppp!" I scream at him laughing.

"Say you're sorry," he demands.

"Never," I fire back.

He continues the punishment. "Say it."

"Okay, okay. I'm sorry." I keep wiggling my body underneath him trying to break free.

"Not good enough," he taunts me and keeps going.

"Ah damn, I'm sorry, Asher. You are the sexiest man in the world."

"Better." He stops tickling me but stays on top. He lowers his body down crushing me under his weight, staying propped up on his elbows. Humor dances in his eyes. It's almost like he looks happy.

My nipples harden from the contact. My skin

tingles. Every part of me feels hot. His perfect lips are so close to mine all I want is for him to kiss me. He looks ready to crush his lips to mine. I inch my face up even closer prepared to taste him. His erection is hard against my pelvis; I lift my hips up to meet his.

He instantly backs off me. I feel the loss of his warm body, and it stings. Then I realize he didn't kiss me the whole time his fingers were working me over.

"I'm going to hop in the shower." His voice growing cold and distant, he turns away and retreats into the bathroom.

I have no idea what caused the drastic change in his attitude. We were laughing and joking around one minute, and the next it was like a bucket of cold water was dumped onto his head. It was a nice change to see that under all the layers of asshole that he had a fun, playful side in him. Hoping I get to see it again, I find myself dozing off before he is out of the shower. Better this way since I'm not willing to see which side of him comes to join me in bed.

****

Thump. Thump. Thump.

My eyes pop open. Startled, I look over to see Asher's side of the bed empty. The sheets are cold and in a perfect place. He never came back to sleep. Slipping out of bed, I walk downstairs toward the noise.

I look around the kitchen waiting for the sound again. *Thump. Thump. Thump.* The noise grows louder from outside the door of his workout room. I've only been inside once, while I was cleaning the house. He has a bunch of machines, weights, and equipment inside, answering my question about how he stays in such good shape.

I push it open to see Asher punching the sandbag, hanging from the ceiling. He's wearing gray sweats, which sit low on his hips. His chest is bare, sweat dripping off him. Every swing he takes is compelling, his muscles rippling from the contact. I watch his abs contract through his heavy breathing. I'm unable to pull my eyes from the sight. He's a work of art and muscle; his punches are graceful and coordinated, his face studying the bag, concentrating where to hit next.

"What do you want, Kylie?" He drops his fists but keeping his face still on the swinging bag. I hadn't realized he knew I was there with his back toward me the entire time.

"I woke up, I heard a noise, and you weren't there."

He turns his attention toward me, finally looking at me. His blue eyes are darker than usual. His chest rises and falls rapidly. That's when I notice the red stain of lipstick on his neck. My chest tightens. "Where were you?" My voice is hard. I barely recognize it.

He stomps toward me, and his heavy footsteps echo off the hardwood floors. He stops in front of me, bringing his face close to mine. The smell of alcohol and cigarettes invades my nose. "That's not how this works here," he spits, "You don't get to ask me where I was."

I push my hands at his chest, "Yes, I do. I sleep in your bed every night. Your fingers were in me only a few hours ago; I have every right to know."

The Asher from earlier is gone. His nostrils flare, lips drawn tight. "You want to know where I went, Kylie?"

No, I don't think I can handle it. "Yes," I answer

anyway.

A cruel smile tugs on his lips, his arms crossed over his chest. I watch the beads of sweat drip down to his abs. I take in a gulp of air, bracing myself for his answer. "I went to a bar and had a few drinks. While I was there, this chick crawled into my lap."

I let out a pained noise and look away as the tears form in my eyes. Asher reaches his tattooed hand out grabbing my jaw, bringing my face up toward him, "You wanted to know. Now you'll let me finish." His grip tightens around me, almost painfully. "So here she is kissing my neck, whispering in my ear how she wanted me to take her home. Promising me I could have her any way that I wanted." He continues, as my heart sinks. "But guess what my sweet little spade, I couldn't do it. Ask me why I couldn't."

He lets my jaw go, so I'm able to speak, "Why?" I choke out.

"Because you're in my fuckin' head. I didn't want her, and it's messed up because I can't keep you!"

My eyebrows draw together in confusion, "What do you mean you can't keep me?"

"Nothing."

"Nothing?" I hiss at him. "That's all you have to say! What if I went out and sat on another man's lap tonight? Then what, Asher?"

His jaw ticks. "I would kill him."

We glare at each other. I feel relieved that he pushed her off him, but I'm still pissed he put himself in that situation. The jealousy made its way into my bones, sinking in thick, and I can't seem to shake it. I shouldn't even be having this reaction. We're not a couple. I don't even know if I like him, yet it still hurts.

"I'm going back to bed," I announce, done with this conversation.

He reaches for me again, but I manage to get past him and run back to his bedroom shutting the door behind me and hitting the lock. Doggy house for you tonight, jerk.

Chapter Thirteen

Kylie

There was an early dismissal at the school today, which I decided to take advantage of and break away from the driver Asher sent me here with this morning. I figure as long as I can make my way back here in time, he won't even realize I was gone. I'm crossing my fingers and wishing for at least.

Hailing a taxi, I hop in and give the driver directions to Tyler's shop. The drive isn't long, but we venture through rougher areas along the way. The streets become littered with people as we get deeper into the city. Some hang outside on their steps with groups of friends, drinking and laughing. Others are blasting loud music, and children are even dancing in the streets enjoying their half a day. We pass homeless men and women, carrying signs and cans filled with change. A few will tap on the window accepting whatever is in the bottom of your pockets. Graffiti lines most of the buildings. I find myself wondering how the artist manages to get up on high spaces creating such amazing works of art. City life has always fascinated me; Blake always used to tell me I was too curious for my good. He found graffiti as a crime and describes it as destroying one's property. He saw the world as black and white or right and wrong, missing all the bright areas in between. I sigh wondering why I didn't end things with him sooner.

The cab begins to slow as we pull up in front of Tyler's shop. The driver, whose nameplate reads Samuel, turns around to face me after reading off the meter. He keeps a picture of his family by the speedometer. Three boys and two little girls with smiling faces stare up at him. I'm not sure if he strategically placed that picture there, but I find myself digging in my bag for extra tip. He thanks me as I open the door and step out.

It's now over four weeks since I've seen Tyler last, and I miss his easy-going attitude. His personality is a welcome change from having been dealing with Chase and Asher lately. He is the fun and light, and they are harsh and dark. I walk through the open garage doors. The shop smells like grease and gas, everything that reminds me of Tyler, and I'm instantly happy.

His shop is a car lover's dream. With two new lifts in the front and every tool, one could ever ask for in large toolboxes. The tile floor is in black and white squares like a checkered racing flag. Tyler designed the garage on his own, and it's perfect for him and his business. Half of which is legit. It's the other half that landed him in jail.

The radio is blasting country music, and I can hear him singing along off key to the tunes. He has his body inside the hood of a red convertible that he is working on.

"Tye." I run up behind his crouched over frame and jump onto his back.

"I was wondering when you were going to get your ass in here to see me." Setting me back down on my feet, he pulls me into a hug.

"I'm sorry. Everything has been crazy," I tell him, which is an understatement. "I missed you. Don't you dare ever leave me alone with Chase again."

He lets out a laugh. "I'm surprised you two haven't killed each other yet." And he's right. I inherited his temper. We are a lot alike. When we clash, it's like world war three.

I sit in the driver's seat of the car with the door hanging open as he continues his work on the engine. It brings me back to when I was younger, and Tyler would come home with a new car. I would lounge in the seats listening to music and bellowing out lyrics, while he would work on, or strip the car apart around me.

At the time, I didn't understand where all the new cars would come from, and every time I asked, he would tell me "it's a friend's." After a few years of the charade, I realized there was no way in hell Tyler's friends were driving around in high-end cars.

"So, how are things going with Asher?" he asks casually.

"As good as you could imagine." One minute he's hot and looking at me like he wants to feast on me, and the next minute he's cold and can't run out the door fast enough.

"He at least treating you right?" He picks his head up from the car and looks at to the side of the popped open hood at me.

I'm not entirely sure how to answer that. If you count giving me the best orgasm I've ever had as right, then I would say he's treating me great. Now, if you count him going to the bar letting a whore crawl on his lap, then he's a dick head.

"Yeah, I mean for the most part we stay out of each other's way." Which is also true, the other night was the closest I've ever gotten to the man, and that ended with him avoiding me even further. I swallow down the sting of rejection.

Tyler stares at me silently deep in thought. I can tell he has something he wants to get off his mind but is afraid to say it. He pops the hood down and sets his tools on the shelf behind him before giving me his full attention. "Just don't get too close to him, Kye."

It isn't because he thinks I'm in any physical danger, but he's worried about me getting attached. He can read me like an open book ever since I was a child. It's like he has this internal bullshit meter that would go off with every fib I told. Unlike Chase, who has never really had a damn clue about what went on inside my head.

"I can handle myself," I tell him without denying anything he is hinting toward. He'll know if I try to lie my way out anyway.

He nods his head not looking convinced but lets the topic of Asher drop. "Have you talked to Blake? I've seen him driving by the house in the patrol car."

My stomach instantly sinks at the sound of hearing his name. I can feel the guilt like it's running through my veins. "No, not since before I left with Asher."

Tyler walks over to the side of the car and gets into the passenger seat next to me. He turns the dial to lower the music before his voice goes soft as he speaks, "I'm sorry you had to do this for me, Kylie." I notice he uses my full name. "I would have never let you make a deal with a man like Asher Black if I was around to control the situation. I realize what you gave up for me. I know

Blake loved you. I may hate his career choice, but that doesn't change that he's a good man. I'd rather see you on his arm than a man like Asher's."

A tear runs down the side of my cheek. I brush it away before he sees. I don't want him to feel worse than he already does. "Chase told me the exact opposite."

He laughs, and I start laughing too. Just like that, the mood is lightened. Tyler has one of those contagious laughs where it's almost impossible ever to have a straight face around him. "And that should tell you enough right there."

We both continue laughing. The sound of my burner phone vibrating in my pocket interrupts us; I pull it out to see "The Devil" is calling. I change his name to that every time he hands me a new phone, and every time he watches me, silently rolling his eyes. Tyler sees my phone screen and raises a brow. I shrug my shoulders and flip the top up.

"Kylie."

"Asher."

"Want to tell me why you aren't at work?" He asks.

"Half day, Dad," I tell him sarcastically, dragging out the dad part.

"Don't, Kylie." His voice threatening, "Where are you?"

"You know where I am." I'm curious to see how good he is. I want to know if he knows everything that is going on.

He laughs. "Of course I do, is the convertible you're sitting in stolen?"

I look around, wondering how the hell he knows

that. "You are such an asshole."

"Aww baby, are you going to give me the silent treatment again? Maybe this time I'll lick your pussy till you submit." His words are always so vulgar.

"No need. Won't be making another mistake again," I snap back.

"We'll see about that; I'm sending a driver to pick you up soon. We're going out to dinner tonight. I have to meet an old friend. Dress nice." He hangs up in a typical Asher Black fashion before I can even ask where.

Chapter Fourteen

Asher

I hang up on Kylie before she starts mouthing off to me. Things have been a little strained between us since I had my hands all over her tight body. I enjoyed the show too much, and before I could do something stupid like kiss her and make her believe something more is going on between us, I did what any other man would do in the situation, and I backed off. I lost control that night. I let her in and showed her a side of me that has been buried for a long time, then I got drunk and said too much. I'm pissed at myself for slipping up. I'm pissed for not being able to use that girl's body to push my thoughts of Kyle away.

She is a means to an end, and we both need that reminder. It's time to pull the whole plan together. She needs to be shown what this is and the kind of person I am, so she doesn't get any ideas about a happy ending with me. It's also time for Blake Owens to see me with her. Killing two birds with one stone, I figure. Kylie will see me for who I am, and Blake will see the emotionless asshole he helped create. I want him to watch me drag her all over the town on my arm. I want him to know I've won the game he started all those years back.

I was shocked when I got a call from the prick. He said he needed to talk, almost making it too easy for me. I know this little meet up is about some bullshit police business. Other than law related shit, we avoid each other altogether. If I'm correct, it's going to be about Hunter Lloyd, but when the opportunity comes knocking, you answer the door.

He wanted me to go to the station. No way was I going back in there willing and being the circus show, while all the cops stare and wait for the beast inside me to lash out. I met my quota of visiting police stations for the month already. Once is more than enough.

That's when I used the opportunity to put my whole plan into motion. I told officer asshole to meet me at a restaurant, Vincenzo's, tonight if he needs to talk to me. He's going to have no idea what hit him when he comes in and I have Kylie dressed up next to me. I hope she wears another tight dress showing off her rack again. I want Owens to know it's me who's going to take her home and play with those tits. I want him to get a taste of his own medicine and choke on it.

It's still early in the day; we aren't expected to meet Owens till tonight, so I make my way to Satin Ladies, the city's biggest nude bar. I have a meeting with the owner about opening another potential strip club on the East End.

I walk in the front door and am met with half naked girls dancing on poles around me. My dick doesn't even respond to the curvy girl wearing nothing but a neon g-string, twirling around. Her eyes go wide taking me in. She shoots me a smile before bending over giving me a view of everything she has to offer. She does absolutely nothing for me. In the past, I would have invited her to a back room. Possibly even a bathroom, where I'd bang her against a wall. I never gave a single thought about the who or the where. If she was ready and willing, then who was I to turn her down? Now nothing stirs inside me in a room with half-naked willing girls. Damn Kylie and her banging body.

"Bill." I walk over to the owner and take a seat next to him at the bar.

He pours me a shot of top-shelf whiskey that I down right away before taking him in. Bill Bishop is a large German man in pretty good shape for pushing fifty. He's watching the girls twirl around the pole with hooded eyes. He barely breaks eye contact with a brunette while she puts on a show, most likely for my benefit. She has no effect on me, but he seems hypnotized by her movements. After doing this for so long, I'm surprised seeing a naked female still does it for him. Not that I give a shit about his sex life. I'm only here for business, and I will admit he knows the strip club game. He's been making a killing owning this one. I know he also thinks it's time he branches out, which is where I come in.

"Black," he greets me. "What do you think of the new girl I just hired?" He points to the brunette that he's been ogling, like a horny teenager with a crush who's hyped up on testosterone.

"Great rack, I'd bend her over," I tell him since that's what he wants to hear. Meanwhile, there's no way in hell I'd even be able to get my dick hard for that girl. Not anymore at least.

Approval is in his eyes. "So I think we could use this kind of talent on the east side of the city."

"I agree, and I want what's rightfully mine." He knows splitting profits with me is the only way this is going to happen. I hope he agrees because I have no desire showing him how I do things. At the end of the day, I will do what needs to be done. Business is business after all.

"I'll cut you in thirty percent of all profits," he offers, and I consider this, but I know he makes a shit ton more money than that. He gets full profit from this one since it's just out of my reach, but if he thinks he's coming into my territory, then he better be willing to pay up.

"Fifty percent or you find a new location."

He pauses thinking about it. His knee is bouncing under the bar; he catches me to glimpse at it before it goes completely still. He's nervous like most people I come in contact with. He also doesn't want to agree, but I know, as well as he does, that he will give in one way or another.

"Did you hear about Hunter Lloyd? He's missing." He pauses taking a swig of his drink. "Word on the street is that you or one of the Turner twins had something to do with it," he says out of the blue.

"Is that right?" I ask him not showing him much reaction to his attempt to bait me. I've heard what everyone has been saying. Conversations always seem to go silent when I enter a room. People like to believe that will stop me from hearing the whispers. From what I've been able to pick up, the poll seems to be divided. Chase is the primary suspect, followed by yours truly. Carrying Kylie out of the Pit that night seemed to have put me on the grid. Either way, if this fucker next to me thinks for one second I'm scared and am going to agree to anything he's offering, he's in for a rude awakening.

"Just saying, people talk Asher, and I don't need that type of shit blowing back on my club. I'm willing to take a chance and give you that thirty percent is knowing that people are gunning for you because I respect the shit out of you, but I'm not sure I have the confidence in handing fifty percent over to you." His knee is at it again, bouncing wildly this time.

There isn't anything but the truth in his statement. I have enemies everywhere. The type that can potentially try to mess with my businesses. I'd never allowed that shit to happen though, and I refuse to have some asshole who gets off on vengeance for his brother's death come between me and my money.

"You claim to respect me, yet here you are questioning me and accusing me. I don't allow personal shit to interfere with my business. The deal is half, or you can take your club to a new location. I'll give you until tomorrow."

I stand up and head for the door. I control the situation always. I don't wait for him or anyone else to dismiss me. Barely back in the truck before my phone is flashing Bishop's name across the screen.

"Fifty percent it is," he says.

I smile and hang up and head home.

Luke Bryan is blasting when I walk into my house. I had no idea who the hell he even was till Kylie moved in. If I ever have to listen to her talk about how he shakes his ass again, I'll have to blow my brains out. It would be nice to have her talking to me on a regular basis, though.

I pull a beer out from the fridge then sit on the couch hoping there's a good football game on so I can drown out the noise from upstairs.

"Ash?" Kylie's voice pulls me from the TV. I turn to look at her, and holy shit she looks good. She's in a tight red dress that stops mid-thigh, with a slit that runs higher. Images of me pushing her up against the wall, hiking her skirt up and burying my cock deep inside her flash through my head.

Her blonde hair is in long curls, and her makeup is dark. She looks more like the type of girl that would be on my arm and less like the type would be with the good old cop. *Perfect.*

"I wasn't sure where we were going tonight. Is this okay?" She is too sweet for a man like me. She's going to despise me when she sees what I have in store for later.

"You're perfect. We need to leave now before I back you against that wall and fuck you till you can't see straight."

Her face turns a shade lighter than her dress. She makes this too much fun for me. I walk up to her and brush my finger down her red cheek. "What no comeback, baby? Is that what you want?"

"No," she says, but it comes out more like a whisper.

I grin at her. "We'll save that for later."

Chapter Fifteen

Kylie

Asher pulls my hand leading me toward an upscale restaurant. When we walk in, the gorgeous hostess greets him by name. Her eyes linger on him a little longer then I care to like. I find myself moving closer to Asher's side. It doesn't go unnoticed by him; he turns toward me shooting me a smug grin. I look away quickly, refusing to acknowledge what just happened there.

There's no wait for Mr. Black as we are escorted to a private booth in the back of the restaurant. This is most likely where he conducts his business. I picture him sitting here eating spaghetti and meatballs in a fancy suit, joined by other mobsters as they talk about taking people out permanently. I choke back a laugh causing Asher to turn around and look at me questioningly. Shrugging my shoulders, I slide into the booth, and he slides in next to me. He orders me a glass of wine and whiskey on the rocks for himself while I contemplate if I watch too many movies.

Before I can ask him who is meeting us, I catch movement in the corner of my eye; instantly I feel all the color from my face drain. The absolute last person I ever expected to see sits in our booth directly across from us. No way could this be happening. I can't breathe. I'm seconds away from going into a full panic attack. Asher's large hand squeezes into my bare thigh under the table warning me to calm down.

Blake's face mirrors my expression when he looks across the table from Asher to me. I'm not the only one who was unaware of this meeting. He fidgets with the collar of his uniform, pulling at it like it's choking him. His face pales. He looks ready to throw up right in front of us. He reluctantly tears his gaze from mine without acknowledging my presence. My heart breaks all over again.

"Officer Owens," Asher greets him with a smirk on his face.

My face whips toward Asher, hair flying in all directions when it hits me. He knew about this. He arranged this whole f thing. I try to rip his hand off my thigh, but his grip tightens. I stare at him with anger and disgust, despising him with every cell in my being. His nails continue to dig into my thigh silently threatening me not to cause a scene.

Blake clears his throat nervously. He's in uniform, so he won't cause a problem. He's always a professional before anything else. His breathing is labored. He's fighting to keep it together, just as much as I am.

"Ash." he says, through gritted teeth. "I have reason to believe you know about the disappearance of Hunter Lloyd." Straight to business, he wants out of here as fast as possible. That makes the two of us.

Asher loosens his grip on my thigh and starts rubbing his fingers softly back and forth on my skin, causing goose bumps to wake in his path. Attempting again, I swat his hand away, but it does no good. The more I attempt to push him away from me, the harder he digs into my skin.

I'm so angry I can't even think straight. I lower my head and watch the tattoos on his hand rub back and forth on my skin; my own hands balled into fists at my sides. My eyes remain focused on my lap as I try to steady my breathing. Act unfazed, put on your best poker face, don't let him win.

"I have no idea who you are referring to," Asher says back confidently. He's calm, not even the slightest trace of the blatant lie coming out of his mouth. I could speak up and tell Blake the truth. I should do it, but I can't manage to get the words out. As much as I hate the bastard, part of me doesn't want him to go back to jail.

He starts rubbing his fingers higher up my thigh. I growl softly only enough for him to hear. He lets out a small laugh and continues his slow journey up my leg.

"Maybe these will help refresh your memory." Blake pulls out a folder. Picking up my head for a second, because I can't fight back the curiosity, I look at the pictures he laid out on the table. They are of Hunter's dead body on the floor of what looks like a bedroom. The room is void of all furniture or anything other than a bed. It seems as if the place is unlived in with the lack of personal touches and plain walls. The wood floors are beautiful I notice, and the room looks clean, the whole thing is strange indeed. Then I take in Hunter, or what was Hunter. Half his body is in bandages from the fight with Chase. There is no fresh blood, or anything damaged around the room to indicate a struggle. Asher chocked him out with his bare hands. That had to be the only way.

I let out a gasp just as the realization occurred to

me, at the same time Asher rubs his fingertip on the lace edges of my thong. Snapping my head in his direction, I glare a hole through him. There's no way he's about to do what I'm thinking.

Both their faces look in my direction. Blake's wears a look of sadness, confusion and hurt, while Asher appears to be calm and confident. He's always in control like the conceded asshole he is.

"You okay? You have goosebumps, baby," Asher says to me with a smug smile on his lips. "Maybe you're cold," he suggests laughing.

Blake's whole body stiffens across the table when Asher calls me baby. He's messing with us both. This is all a game to him.

"I'm fine," I growl at Asher narrowing my eyes at him.

He runs his finger up the center of my panties. I shiver at his touch; my nails dig into the booth cushion. I hate him. I hate more that I feel myself getting wet, my body responding to his touch, in a restaurant across from my ex-boyfriend.

Asher winks at me and returns his attention to the picture, studying it as if he can't place it. "I think I've seen him at the Pit a few times. He's normally livelier there than in these pictures." He laughs at his joke. He freaking laughs.

His fingers push aside my thong, grazing across my bare flesh. I keep my head down and bite my tongue to hold back any noises. My body is turned on. I'm practically soaking and he knows it too, now. I'm disgusted with myself.

Blake has no idea what is going on right in front of him, underneath the table. He would never have treated me this way. Asher remains completely unaffected by all of it. Almost looking bored while I'm on the verge of an orgasm, and Blake seems as if he'd rather be Hunter right now.

I can hear Blake talking, but I can't focus on what he is saying. I'm concentrating on keeping my mind off the climax that is building while Asher's finger finds my clit and draws circles. I shiver when he starts lightly pushing his finger into my core. I'm a prisoner to my desire. I can't help how good it feels, how good his touch is on my body, and how much I crave him even though the whole situation is wrong.

"Baby, I think you need some water. You look a little flushed." Asher directs the attention back to me.

"I'm fine." My voice is strained coming through my clenched teeth. I keep my head down not giving him the satisfaction of seeing the lust on my face.

I can hear the muffled voices again picking up words here and there. I understand something about Hunter's brother asking questions and out for revenge, but I can't focus on anything going on around me the closer I get to fighting myself from falling off the edge.

I didn't notice Blake leave when I feel Asher biting on my ear. "He's gone." He quickens his pace.

"Please stop." I fight back moans.

"You like when I rub my fingers in your pussy in front of your ex?"

"NO." *Yes*.

"No? You're soaked." He sounds angry with me.

"Screw you."

"This is mine now, baby. Stop fighting me."

He bites down on my neck, and my body clenches around his fingers as the orgasm rocks through me. It's strong from how much I tried to fight it back.

Asher kisses the tears away that escaped my eyes. I failed at fighting them back too.

He keeps his lips by my ear, and his voice goes cold. "That's the last time you will ever get turned on in front of another man. You will not fuck him again. I ruined him for you. Every time you look at his face, you will think about my fingers in your body. I own you now."

The tears continue to fall down my face as we eat together in silence. He was right. He ruined Blake for me.

Chapter Sixteen

Kylie

"I'm going out tonight," I yell to Asher on my way out the door. I don't make it down the porch before he's behind me, grabbing my arm stopping me.

"Where the hell are you going?" he asks annoyed. "And nice attempt."

"Find me if you want to know, you're good at that." I rip my arm from him and get into his driver's car.

I tell him to take me to the Pit. Chase is fighting again tonight, and I know Tyler will be there to protect me if shit goes sour again.

It's been a week since the incident at the restaurant. This time, instead of ignoring him, I've thrown my attitude at him at full speed. I'm disgusted with the show he put on. I refuse to be part of his twisted games. Every time I close my eyes, I see Blake's face laced with confusion and sadness. I have no idea where the intense hate Asher has for Blake stems from. Then again, I'm not aware of many criminals who befriend cops other than the crooked ones, which Blake isn't.

My mind swirls with thoughts about that night. The anger I felt is still lying dormant inside of me, but underneath it all is curiosity. I was able to get off in public, in front of my ex. I shouldn't have been turned on, yet I was drenched. I can't deny the lust I feel for

Asher anymore. He tempts me to throw caution to the wind, daring me to be the wild person who gets off in a restaurant by the hands of a man who can snap someone in half. The confusion stirs in me when Asher is around. My body wants him, but in my head, I know he's not a nice person. I'm entirely torn in half. I want to stay away from him. I should keep my distance, but I can't. I get pulled into his intense gaze. His edginess and mysteriousness draw me in. Like a curious little kitten. We haven't even had sex yet, and I'm already twisted up inside because of him.

Tonight, I had to get away from him before I let the anger and passion explode inside me. There is a fine line between the two when it comes to him. If either side wins, the outcome is going to be a disaster.

Tyler is waiting outside the Pit smoking a cigarette when I pull up. His eyes go light when he sees me. He opens his arms for me to walk into them. I sigh into his chest, loving the feel of Tyler's bear hugs.

"Look at you going from rags to riches." He nods to the retreating limo.

"Shut up." I roll my eyes at him and hold back my laugh. "Who's he fighting tonight?"

"Big Ben, remember him? I think I caught you two making out behind the bleacher freshman year."

"Oh my God you're kidding." Now I'm hysterically laughing. I do remember him, and I think he pissed himself when Chase and Tyler caught us. Finding a date was pretty hard in high school with two crazy bodyguards threatening every guy who even looked in my direction.

"It's about time one of us gets to kick his ass." Tyler punches the air with his fists and hops around on his toes. He looks ridiculous and more like he's hopscotching than boxing.

"Tyler!" I laugh punching his arm, "We were like fourteen at the time!"

"Doesn't matter! You're still my annoying little sister." He throws his arm around me as we head down the steps into the Pit basement.

I'm glad to be comfortable tonight, wearing jeans, a tee, and my white sneakers. The crowd tonight is almost double the size from last time. The afterword about Chase's previous fight got out, everyone wanted in on the action, and here they are hoping for some more drama. Tyler guides me through the sea of bodies. I'm grateful to have him on my arm.

"Why is everyone looking at us?" Tyler leans down and whispers in my ear. I hadn't noticed, but now looking around I can tell people are looking at me. A few have even backed away from me.

Then I figure it out. "Last time the infamous Asher Black carried me out of here." I roll my eyes.

"You're like a local celebrity now," he teases me bowing down. "Right this way, Princess Kylie."

As we walk up to Chase, he's surrounded yet again by girls. Tyler removes his arm from my shoulder and pushes me out of the way. He takes his now free arms and wraps them around two girls talking to Chase.

"Asshole!" I glare at him.

He turns his head around and winks at me. I stick my tongue out at him because I'm mature like that, and it's followed by the fun sound of his laughter.

I make my way over to the makeshift bar set up tonight. I order myself and Tyler bottles of beer. There isn't a choice of anything else here. It's beer or beer. I wouldn't want to be caught dead sipping on a martini the middle of a fight. That's one way to look like easy prey.

Movement out of the corner of my eye catches my attention. A stocky man wearing a red hood is walking through the crowd looking around curiously. I pay the bartender for the beer as my eyes follow the stranger. I look back at Chase and Tyler still drowning in girls then again to the man. He seems to be looking for something or someone. Chills run down my spine. I get a *deja vu* feeling of the man who handed Hunter the knife. Could it be?

Before I can even register what I'm doing, I follow him down the hallway that leads to the bathrooms. It's like my feet have a mind of their own and keep pressing forward. The strange man is walking fast almost like he knows he's being followed. I try and tell my brain to stop and turn around, but I'm unable to bring myself to do it. Curiosity is stirring in the back of my mind, nagging at me like an itch that needs to be scratched. The need to know if it is Hunter's brother outweighs any common sense I have. I continue following trying to stay hidden behind the crowd of people. I follow till he makes a right at the end of the hallway. When I get to the end, I look to the right, and he's gone. The hall is deserted, a strange sense of feeling creeps over me, as I shiver.

The chills continue to run through my body. My mind is on high alert. I turn around to head back as a hand reaches out grabbing me by my arm roughly and pulling me into the darkness. The man with the hood is standing in my face. I look into his cold dead eyes as fear shoots through me, riddling me to my core. I begin shaking, unable to get my body under control. He pushes my back against the wall locking his hand over my mouth. I look up again at his face, and I know he is who I thought he was. This face has been plastered all over the news. He is Logan Lloyd, Hunter's brother.

When the shock begins wearing off and I'm able to move again, I claw at his hand covering my mouth. I cling to the thought of fighting him off. Chase and Tyler raised me that way. He is too strong for me, though. He slams my head back against the wall.

"Stop fighting me, bitch." He spits in my face. "I know one of your brothers or your boyfriend killed my brother."

I'm trying to shake my head back and forth to tell him no. I can feel the tears running down my face. He's going to kill me. He has that look in his eyes. Manic.

"I'm going to take my hand away, if you scream I will end you."

I gasp for air when he releases my mouth. The oxygen couldn't make its way back into my lungs fast enough. The ache in my neck throbs. My body starts to fall forward but is caught by his forearm as he pushes me up straight back against the wall. The knife in his hand is dangerously close to my face.

"Who killed him?"

"I-I d-d-don't kn-know," I stutter.

He slaps me hard across the face with his free hand. I can feel blood running down my cheek. I shake my head as much as I can before the knife hits my face. I would never rat on Asher. My body swells with protectiveness for him no matter what this asshole does to me; I won't talk. I would rather die than give up any information about someone I care for.

"Tyler was locked up that leaves Chase or Asher! Tell me or they both die." He screams in my face. Spit flies out of his mouth landing on me. His forearm digging into the flesh of my neck is the only thing keeping me from gagging.

"Neither of them," I say through sobs.

He hits me again, this time I feel my lip bust open. "Tell me, bitch!" His frustration grows the more I don't answer. He isn't far off from digging the blade in and carving out my face.

He lifts his other hand to slap me again, but a group of guys laughing at the end of the hallway stops him. He puts his finger up to his lips telling me to shush. He slowly backs away from me letting my body slump to the ground. Then just like he appeared, he's gone.

I'm too terrified to move. Scared that if I get up, he will be there waiting for me. Reaching into my pocket, I pull my phone out and scroll till I find "The Devil." I don't know why in a panic state I choose him to call, but he was the first person that popped up in my head. Maybe subconsciously I do understand why. I can't deny that he makes me feel safe.

He answers on the first ring, "Kylie."

I sob into the phone. I can't even speak.

"I'm coming, baby." Then he hangs up.

Chapter Seventeen

Asher

I hang up on Kylie. She couldn't even form words as I listened to her sobs coming through the phone. The second I hang up, I chug back the last shot of whiskey in my hand before smashing the glass against the wall. The shattered glass over the wood floors of my office causes my boots to make a crunching noise every step I take. I curse the air around me; I'm livid because they were supposed to watch her. I know she's at The Pit with her brothers. If there is a piece of hair out of place on her head, I'm going to kill them.

I hop into my truck and speed to the Pit, not giving a shit how many red lights I blow on the way. Half the cops in this city are in my pocket. The other half wouldn't dare screw with me, except for Owens.

The crowd is chanting loud for Chase when I walk in. I push past everyone who stands in my way till I find Tyler with two girls on his arms. I walk up to him, wrap my hand around his neck, and take him to the ground.

"Where is she?" I scream at him.

He grasps for breath, trying to fight me off him, which makes me squeeze harder instead. A crowd forms around us. I don't notice the fight has stopped until Chase tackles me off Tyler.

"Where is she?" I ask again, and the two dip shits

start looking around realizing they have no clue where their sister is.

"She was right here a few minutes ago!" Tyler says, raspy.

"Yeah well, why did she call me sobbing then stupid ass." I'm up in his face again, forcing my closed fists to stay at my sides.

Chase steps in front of Tyler and gets in my face. "Back away, Asher."

"I don't have time to deal with your shit. Help me find your sister," I bark at them.

Reluctantly Chase backs down. Finally, his face grows worried letting it sink in that finding his sister is more important than the bullshit between us. He walks up to different people, half scaring the shit out of them, to ask if they've seen her.

Minutes pass as we continue walking around the crowd searching for her. It feels like a lifetime before we get any piece of information. Tyler, who had been talking to the guy at the bar, calls us over. He asks the short chubby man with thick-framed glasses to repeat what he told him. The man looks like he's about to piss his pants while looking up at the three of us towering over him. In a nervous voice, he tells us he saw her go toward the back hallway that leads to the bathrooms.

I make my way into the hallway with Chase and Tyler trailing me. The noise of sobs coming from the end of the hall has my heart racing. The sound gets louder the farther down we move. I turn the corner and take one look at her before I see red.

She's slumped over with her back pressed against the wall. There are fresh tears and blood dripping from her face. Her white tee is stained with blood and ripped open. She has her knees curled up to her chest with her arms wrapped around them. I have seen too many tears fall from her beautiful face in the past few weeks. Guilt tugs at my cold heart.

Chase and Tyler run to each side of her. Tyler pulls her into his chest as Chase demands her to tell him who did this. I already know who is responsible for this. My blood is boiling. I feel the beast within gnawing to come out. He won't be satisfied till he's had his revenge.

"Hunter's brother." Tears continue down her face, dripping to her ripped shirt.

I lose the remaining self-control I had. I punch the wall next to me, sending my fist straight through the drywall. My knuckles burn, but it doesn't stop me from doing it again.

"Calm the hell down! You're scaring her." Tyler gets up stopping me from my rage. His eyes narrow at me. "She doesn't need to see this."

Both he and Chase glare at me.

"Leave, both of you." I snap at them, done with their presence.

Chase gets up and is back in my face. "No chance. She's coming home with us." He crosses his arms over his chest.

"Like hell she is. Where were you two when this was happening? It's too late now. She called me. *Now leave!*"

Inches are separating us, neither backing down. The only reason I haven't hit him is that Kylie is still pissed at me from last week. I didn't mean to let things go that far that night. I'll admit I got carried away. I couldn't help myself once Blake was in my presence. A surge of possessiveness came over me. I had to make sure that she would never run back to him. The need to claim her blocked out any rational thought. I've been paying for that dick move all week. She hasn't cooked for me once. One morning I asked her if there was extra and threw a frying pan at my head.

"Go." I hear her say softly causing Chase to whip his head back to her wearing a shocked expression.

"Kylie you don't want to come with us?" he speaks softly to her.

"Please go," she tells them again, which surprises me. She loves those crazy fucks more then I'll ever understand, but now she's choosing me when it matters.

Tyler kisses her on the head, "I'm so sorry, baby girl." He gets up and pulls a fuming Chase away with him. I hear Chase fighting him and calling me a few choice words until the end of the hallway.

I look back down at her and start counting numbers in my head, to calm down, before I go to her. I take a step closer, and she tries to back away farther into the wall. I feel my chest squeeze knowing that she's still afraid of me.

"Baby, I won't hurt you," I tell her not sure my word means shit after what I did last week, but this is different.

I never would physically lay a hand on her. I may get a little rough sometimes and do a ton of questionable shit, but I would never hurt a woman. Rapist and wife beaters are the scum of the earth.

I kneel in front of her and put my fingers under her chin to make her look at me. I hiss when I see her cheek is split open and her bottom lip is split. Bruises are lightly forming on Kylie's pale skin of her neck.

Lightly I trail my fingers over them. She shivers underneath my touch.

"I'm going to kill him." Not sure if I'm saying that to her or myself, but he will pay for this. He's going to be joining his brother shortly.

"Asher, please get me out of here."

I scoop her up into my arms. I feel her blood and tears soaking into my shirt. I'm used to having blood ruining my clothes. I'm just not used to giving a damn about the person it's coming from.

I carry her like a baby out of the Pit for the second time.

Once we're back at the house, Kylie is still shaking in my arms. I'm fuming at the thought of that bastard putting his hands on her. I carry her to the bathroom and sit her on the lid of the toilet seat then walk over to the bathtub. I turn the water on before running my hands through it checking the temperature. I've never taken care of anything before besides myself. Not even a pet. The feeling is unknown to me.

Kylie sits there watching me silently. I kneel in front of her and untie the sneakers on her feet, pulling them off one by one. Standing her up, I begin to unbutton her pants, but stop to look up at her. When she doesn't say anything or object, I continue undressing her till she's naked and beautiful in front of me. I mentally tell my dick to reel it in, but I can't help the bulge trying to break out of my jeans.

Lifting her naked body up, I slowly drop her into the now filled tub, grabbing a washcloth I wipe the blood off her face. She lets out a hiss when I get close to the cuts.

I try to keep my calm when all I want to do is find

the piece of shit and rip him apart limb from limb.

"Tell me exactly what happened," I demand, a little too harshly.

She takes in a deep breath and speaks softly, "I had a feeling he was the guy who handed Hunter the knife at the fight. I thought if I got close enough to him I could be completely sure, and I would have gotten one of my brothers. I guess he knew I was following him, so he leads me down the hallway. When I thought he disappeared, he came out of nowhere and threw me up against the wall screaming at me asking if it was you or Chase who killed his brother."

"Shit." This is my fault, and I'm pissed the hell off about it. Getting up from the edge of the tub I pace around the bathroom.

"What did you say to him?" I hope she told him it was me. I want him to know. Good luck to him if he thinks he can come after me.

"I told him it was neither of you." I look over to her. She looks small in the tub. Her legs are wrapped up tight in her arms, and her face is swollen and streaked with tears. The feeling of guilt is setting in slowly, as an unwelcome foreign guest. I can barely stand looking at her knowing this is my fault. After all the shit I've done to her, and on top of that, she still didn't rat me out.

"You protected me?" I question her. Why she would do that makes no sense.

"Yeah."

"Why?"

"I don't want you to get hurt." Such a simple answer and yet it weighs even heavier on me. I don't even deserve to be in the same room as her. Her loyalty still amazes me. She makes me feel proud knowing that she will have my back even after I give her my worst.

Walking back over to her and sitting on the edge of the tub, I reach over and brush her wet hair away from her face. I lean into her and brush my lips against hers lightly. This is the first time I'm allowing myself to kiss her fully. Her plump lips have been tempting me since the moment she opened her smart little mouth at the poker table. I've fought the urge too long, and after tonight, nothing is stopping me from really tasting her.

She lets out a soft moan and slips my tongue through her parted lips exploring the inside of her mouth. She wraps her arms around my neck and pulls me halfway into the water with her. I kiss her with the anger I have in my body tonight. I suck on her bottom lip and take it between my teeth and nibble. A coppery taste from the blood of the cut on her lip hits the inside of my mouth. Being the sick man that I am, it turns me on a little more.

Water is spilling out onto the tile around us. My shirt is soaked and clinging to my body. My cock is hard, and I know I should stop after what went down tonight, but I can't pull myself away. I look down at her wet body, running my hands up and down her back. I reach my hand around the back of her thigh and brush my fingers lightly through her slit. She starts thrashing her hips in the water. She looks lost in lust. I brush her pussy again before watching confusion take over her features.

She quickly pushes me away from her and backs her body up into the back of the tub. "No. I still hate you."

I can see it written all over her face. She's disgusted with me. She's even more pissed that her body wants me when her mind hates me. I deserve everything she throws at me. The night at the restaurant was only a tiny preview of the game. I would even call it the calm before the shit storm. The gust of wind before the hurricane that will sweep through and leave destruction behind when she finds out who I am to Blake.

I walk out the door without looking back, "There's pain meds in the cabinet. Take one before you go to sleep."

Then I leave.

Chapter Eighteen

Asher

"What took you so long?"

It's after two a.m. I let myself into the Turners house. Not bothering to knock or announce myself. That's not how I work at nighttime. Tyler is sitting on the old worn in couch casually, watching the enormous flat screen TV on the wall. Underneath the TV sits multiple gaming systems. I shake my head at the brand-new electronics in a house that looks like it hasn't been updated since 1940.

I step in front of him placing my body directly in front of his vision. He doesn't look up at my face; instead, he tries looking around my imposing frame. Giving up he lets out a breath of air and stands. Without giving him time to react, my fist connects with his face.

"Shit." His body falls back. Once he recovers from the first hit, he stands straight up again, not bothering to lift a hand to defend himself.

I punch him once more in the stomach, and he falls to the ground. I step over his body, with one down one more to go. "Where is Chase?"

"In his…" Cough. "Room with a girl," Tyler spits out, through coughing.

I throw the bedroom door open like it's my house. Chase is on the bed naked with a girl bouncing on top, riding his dick. His head shoots to me, standing in the doorway. He's not at all shocked by my presence, either.

"Babe, go home," he tells the girl.

She gets up and scrambles around for her clothes. Gathering them, she shoots out the door still naked.

Chase jumps off the bed before picking up a pair of shorts off the floor and throwing them on. "Who do you think you are?" He gets in my face and shoves me into the wall.

I take a swing at him and land a punch straight to his eye. Unlike Tyler, he doesn't back down, and I don't expect him to. This is what I came here for.

I'm pissed at them for leaving her unattended. They knew there was the threat of Logan out there. I'm pissed at myself for allowing her to get hurt. I made the mistake of thinking her brothers would protect her when I wasn't around to do so. That's what led me here tonight. I don't care if he kicks my ass or I kick his. I welcome the pain right now like a good blowjob after weeks of drought.

Chase is back in my face. This time he throws a punch at my ribs. I wince at the pain for a second before I use my shoulder and barrel into his chest. We both fly into the bed. I have him pinned beneath me as I swing at his face over and over again.

He pushes me back onto the floor sending the lamp next to the bed flying. The roles have reversed, and now he has me pinned to the floor throwing his fist to my face. This goes on for what feels like hours, neither one of us backing down.

We're both breathing heavy. There's blood pouring out of our knuckles and streaked across his face. I'm not even sure who it belongs to. I notice a rib is cracked when I take in a deep inhale. It hurts like a bitch to move. I'm ready for this to be over. I reach up and wrap my hand around his throat.

"Enough!" Tyler yells, walking into the room. Well, what's left of the room since half of Chase's shit is shattered on the floor.

We both ignore him. Chase keeps hitting me, and I continue to tighten my grip around his neck.

Tyler gets in the middle of us. He's almost as big as us. Using his strength, he dislodges my hand from Chase's throat, then pulls Chase off and throws him on the ground causing him to land on his ass. "I said enough."

"You should have been watching her." I wipe my mouth on my sleeve, streaking it with blood.

"Yeah, we know that. Don't you think we feel bad enough?" He cradles his jaw with his hand. His eyes are full of regret.

"Asshole! Walks the fuck in here like he owns the place!" Chase paces then tries to lunge at me again, but Tyler throws him back down.

"I swear to God if something like this happens again when she's with one of you, I will bury you." I point to them. "She's mine! I don't give a damn if you're her blood, I'll still take great joy in watching you suffer."

Tyler holds his hands up. "Maybe you should stop and think why she was put in this position in the first place. I sure as hell didn't kill Hunter, and I know Chase didn't kill Hunter, so you do the math…" he trails off.

"Leave it," I tell him, even though he's right. This is my fault.

"Get out of here!" Chase's voice bounces off the walls as he still tries to pass Tyler and get to me.

Chapter Nineteen

Kylie

The sound of the front door opening wakes me up from my medicine-induced sleep. The steps creak under the weight of the person moving up them. I hear an "umpf" noise each time a new step is reached. A few minutes later, I see a large shadow moving awkwardly into the bedroom.

In the dark, I can tell it's Asher by his broad shoulders. Even in the pitch black, his light blue eyes are glowing. He catches me sitting up on the bed watching him struggle to move forward. Without a word, he walks into the bathroom closing it shut behind him. Getting up, I walk over to the bathroom door and knock.

"Not now, Kylie." He speaks loudly over the sound of the running water. Ignoring him, I throw the door open. Feeling sorry about how I dismissed him earlier tonight.

He's sitting on the shower bench with his head down, resting on the palm of his hands. He looks defeated. There's blood dripping off his body into the water, turning it red. He looks like hell. One eye is swollen shut, and there's a huge bruise forming over his ribs.

I turn and look at myself in the mirror. My eyes are puffy from crying, and I have a handprint outline bruise around my neck. There's a gash on my cheek and another on my lip.

I laugh out loud at the sight, and Asher picks his head up. I probably look like I've lost my mind. I feel like I've lost my mind.

"Look at us. We make quite the pair." I say to him, "What happened to you?"

"Your brothers happened."

Nodding my head, I understand why he went there, not that I agree with it.

I begin to strip out of my clothes. Asher watches me with a hungry look in his eyes. Once I drop my thong to the ground, I kick it out of the way with my foot and join him in the shower.

The steam hits my face instantly warming my body, which already feels on fire from Asher's intense gaze.

When he walked out the door earlier, I started thinking about the way he rushed to me when I needed him. The way he took care of me when I was hurt. He defended me when he thought my brothers should have. Then I thought about the haunted look in his beautiful blue eyes when I pushed him away and told him I hated him.

Something changed in me, like a switch was flipped and I decided to let my anger go. I can't fight the feelings I have for him anymore. I'm ready to embrace the darker side of myself that I've been hiding since my relationship started with Blake.

Asher is a taste of the wild that I've been avoiding. I can't run from it anymore. I can't live my life wondering what it could be like to let my guard down with him. He showed me he could be caring. He taught me he could be soft. There isn't anything sweeter than when a hard man becomes soft for the woman he cares about.

Reaching for his hand in the shower, I gently pull him up to stand with me. Once he's up, I wrap my arms around his naked waist and press my face into his hard chest.

The warm water is running over us. I feel at peace in this moment. The first taste of calmness I've had all night. We stay wrapped up in each other's arms for I don't know how long before Asher breaks the silence.

"I was scared when you called me tonight."

"I know." I squeeze my arms tighter around him.

"No, Kylie, you don't. It's been a long time since I gave a shit about anyone. The minute I heard you crying, I lost it. Almost killed your brothers tonight. I can't handle anyone putting their hands on you."

"I'm okay now. I'm fine, Asher, because of you."

He presses his lips to the top of my head. Reaching around me, he pulls open the glass door and steps out. After wrapping a towel around his delicious waist, he holds one out for me. I step into it. Grabbing my hand again, he pulls me toward the bed.

I drop my towel to the floor and scoot back onto the bed. Asher looks down at my body splayed out for him. His eyes are hungry, and he's biting his lip in the sexiest way possible. Making me want to lick and suck on those lips.

"You're beautiful," he says, lust filling his eyes.

"Come over here," I demand impatiently, squirming on the bed.

The smile that takes over his face is gorgeous. Possibly the first time I've seen him look anything but dangerous. The second I feel his hard body climb on top of mine I lose it. I open my thighs wide to accommodate his size. My arms loop around the back of his neck as I pull him in for a hungry kiss.

His hands run up and down my body, leaving nothing untouched and every bit of my skin on fire. Droplets of water run down his neck. I catch them with my tongue, causing him to groan.

There is no going slow tonight. My body is craving his in a way I've never experienced in my life. I'm wet and needy, and Asher is the only man who can give me what I want.

Reaching between us, I wrap my hand around his hard dick. I squeeze him tightly as a moan escapes his lips. I pump my fist faster, watching his face grow hungrier.

"Babe, I'm going to come if you keep doing that." He pries my greedy hand away from his cock, then flips us over so that I'm on top, straddling his waist.

"Move up and sit on my face," he demands.

"No, I can't do that!" I tell him embarrassed, feeling my cheeks go red.

"Babe, sit on my face, now." He growls this time.

I would be lying if I wasn't turned on like crazy from his harsh demanding words. I reluctantly climb up his body till my thighs are on each side straddling his face.

He brings one of his large hands around to each side of my waist, digging his fingers in, holding me still. The second I feel him reach up and lick my slit I scream out. He continues running his tongue up and down driving me wild, devouring me. If it weren't for him holding me tightly, I'd be rotating my hips rapidly against his mouth.

"Let go, baby." He covers my clit with his lips and starts sucking lightly. That's all I need before I'm screaming out his name, and an intense orgasm rocks my body.

Chapter Twenty

Asher

The taste of Kylie in my mouth is like pure heaven. I flip her over onto her back. Her big green eyes look sated. I reach over and pull out a condom from the nightstand.

"We're not done, baby." We are far from done.

"Fuck me, Asher," she says, looking up at me. I can see the desire pouring out of her eyes. She wants me to take her as much as I want to.

She doesn't need to tell me twice. I slip the condom on and settle in between her parted thighs. Rubbing my cock up and down her wet pussy, she shutters, and I push my hard cock into her in one swift motion. She's tight around me. The back of her heels are digging hard into my ass, and her nails are clawing at my back.

I lean my forehead down to hers then thrust my hips into her hard. Her moans are enough to set me off. I've been waiting to get inside her for weeks. I want it to last.

"Ahh Asher, you feel so good," she screams loud enough to wake the neighbors down the street.

I slam into her harder. Thrusting my hips, giving her everything and she takes it all. We're both covered in sweat, breathing loudly. Keeping up the pace, I drive into her tight little body over and over, and the sound of our bodies slapping against each other fills the room.

"Come for me again, baby." At my command, I can feel her body is close. I change my position, so I know I'm hitting the spot with my dick that drives her wild.

"Oh, God!" I feel her tightening around me. A surge of wetness drips out of her pussy, making my dick slide farther in.

"No God, just me." I grin, almost ready to let go. I look down at her beautiful tits bouncing each time I pound my hips into her, and that does it. My cock pulses inside of her, and I collapse my body onto her tiny frame.

We lie like that for a few minutes. Lifting my body up still inside of her. I take in her blonde hair fanned out on my pillow and heavy, happy, sated eyes. She never looked better.

"Sleep, my sweet spade." I reach down and pull my dick out of her holding onto the condom.

Walking into the bathroom, I flip on the light. My eyes take a second to adjust. It isn't till I'm reaching down to take the condom off my limp dick that I realize it broke. Ripping off what's left of the condom, I throw it into the trash bin. Turning toward the mirror, I stare at my reflection contemplating what I should do next.

Part of me knows the right thing to do would be to wake her ass up right now and take her to the store for whatever that plan b shit is. That is what I would do if I were a right person, but the devil sitting on my shoulder is telling is me that this would be the sweetest revenge I could ever dish out. I watch a slow smile appear on my face through the mirror. In that minute, I don't even recognize the monster staring back at me. I've killed, lied, and cheated, but purposely knocking up Kylie would be the worst thing I've done in my criminal life.

My legs carry me back out into the bedroom on autopilot. I look over at Kylie passed out naked on her stomach on top of the sheets. She took pain pills earlier, and since she came twice tonight, she's dead to the world. I softly run my fingers through the inside of her thigh she lets out a soft moan in her sleep. She's soaked still. I can see that some of it is from me. I thought how she looked after we fucked was the best sight to see, but I was wrong. Seeing my cum dripping out of her pussy is the sexiest image I could ever ask for.

Sitting on the chair next to the bed, I watch her sleep, not trying to be a total creep but she looks peaceful. I'm a complete asshole for ruining her life because of the game's between me and Blake. She is an innocent dragged into a feud that she knows nothing of. A dispute that only four people know—me, my father, Blake, and my dead wife.

People don't know that when my wife got pregnant, I was still very much serving my time in jail. People don't know that the baby was never mine. The baby was Blake's. I was in prison while he was sleeping with my wife behind my back. Not even being careful while doing it.

Kylie stirring on the bed pulls me from my haunting memories. She's turned facing away from me. I watch her throw her hand out to my empty side of the bed and move it back and forth searching for me.

"Ash," she whispers in her sleep, and I'm up slipping into the bed next to her. I pull her to my side where she fits perfectly.

"I'm here, baby."

She relaxes into me and falls back into a peaceful sleep. Just like that, my decision is made. I won't tell her. Maybe nothing will happen or perhaps she will be knocked up with my kid. She'll never forgive me for this. Darkness falls over me fast. Guess it won't even keep me up at night.

Chapter Twenty-One

Kylie

My head is throbbing when I wake up in the morning, but I still can't control the smile breaking out on my face from my night with Asher. It was as if the dreadful first half of the night never happened. He took the pain away. He made me feel safe again.

Reaching over to his empty side of the bed its cool, I'm caught wondering how long ago he left. Pulling myself out of bed I head to the bathroom, my face is swollen even more today, but I look different. I seem happier then I have felt in a long time. I finally feel alive, but I'm still in a daze at the events that took place last night.

Applying makeup to cover the marks on my neck is a lost cause, so I opt for a scarf. I pair it with a plain tight-fitting T-shirt and jeans. The outfit makes me look comfortable, yet casual.

"Asher?" I call out into the empty house. Nothing but silence answers. I pick up the new burner phone left on the kitchen table and dial his number.

"Kylie," he answers, sounding distant.

"Um hi, where are you? You were gone when I woke up."

"Florida, had business to attend to."

Florida?

"Are you serious, right now?" I yell into the phone.

"Yeah, I'll be back in a few days," he says, casually. As if picking up and fleeing the state out of nowhere is no big deal. Especially after the night we shared.

The noise of the phone line going dead infuriates me. He's doing it again, pulling away from me the second he gets close. We move one step forward, and he takes three steps back. I woke up feeling great about my life for the first time since I came to stay with him. I thought we were finally in a happy place. I guess I was wrong.

The caring man I had last night is gone. The one who held me and took care of me when I needed him fell right back into his old self. I'm pissed at myself for believing he had changed and was falling for me. He didn't care about me. He got me in bed as he wanted then fled before I ever woke up.

I'm so angry I pick up the phone and send him a text, SCREW YOU. Feeling better, I put the phone down on the kitchen table and leave it there. Grabbing my mug of freshly made coffee, I head to school for the day.

The school day comes and goes fast. I'm glad for that. Keeping busy is the best way to keep my mind from dealing with reality. The fact I let a dangerous man take me to bed. A man who I finally gave entirely in to. A man I shouldn't want but can't seem to let go of. By the time I get back to Asher's house, I have five texts and a missed call.

Asher: Kylie.

Asher: What is your problem?

Asher: ANSWER YOUR PHONE. SHIT.

Asher: I HAD SHIT TO DO HERE. I DON'T

CARE HOW MAD YOU ARE AT ME, YOU BETTER ANSWER.

Asher: Why do I even bother to get you a phone? You have no clue how they work.

Me: Leave me alone.

I write a quick response back. I have entirely no tolerance for his bullshit right now. He's lucky I even replied to him. The only reason I did is that of the threat Logan has put on me. Yeah, I'm pissed, but it would be unfair for him to think something has happened to me. A new message comes in a second later.

Asher: Wait till I get home.

Anger shoots through me from his text. He's an asshole for threatening me. If he thinks I'm just going to let this go, then he's in for a surprise. He wanted me to trust him this whole time then he pulls this shit. No thank you. I'm pissed off that he would leave at a time like this. Hunter's brother knows what I look like now. He knows who I am, and he knows that one of the three men in my life had something to do with his brother's murder.

Scrolling to the missed call, I see Chase's name pop up. Hitting send, I call him back.

"Yo," Chase answers.

"Hey, sorry. I forgot my phone at home today."

"It's cool. What you up to Friday night?"

"Stephanie and Ashley have been asking me to go out with them for weeks. Since Mr. Moody is away, we are going to hit club silver."

Stephanie and Ashley are two of the other teachers from school. I've spent all my time with my brothers growing up I didn't have many girlfriends, but they would be the two closest things I have.

"You said Steph's going?" I roll my eyes. Chase met Steph a few times. She's ignored every attempt he has thrown at her to get in her pants. He's not used to being turned down, and I know it drives him crazy that she won't give in.

"Yes, and no you're not going anywhere near her," I tell him.

He laughs. "Come on that's not fair. I'm a good guy."

Pshh, "You're a great guy. When it comes to women, you're a pig."

"I'm hurt and offended Kylie, and with that, I'll see you Friday night. Peace." He hangs up.

Great. I sigh.

Chapter Twenty-Two

Asher

I find myself pacing outside of Florida State Penitentiary walls, trying to gain the balls to walk inside. Bringing a cigarette to my lips, I take a long drag, calming me for a few seconds till I exhale the smoke from my lungs. The reason I came here, why Kylie is giving me shit, is sitting on the other side. It's been years since I've seen the man. Years since I've even spoken to him. The only place in the world that I avoid going back inside. The only place that makes me feel trapped is the only place I will ever get to see him, alive at least.

I ran this morning. Ran away fast and hopped on the first flight to Florida. The decision was impulsive, but I needed time to clear my head after last night. I don't even know that made me come here. It just seemed like a good idea at the time. Now I'm wondering what the hell I was thinking.

Owen Black is the first name I see on the visitors sign in sheet once I've gained the courage to go inside. His name is the only one I see in all three pages until mine now.

"Black." The stocky guard calls me. He has that tough guy air about him. He looks me up and down taking me in. Yeah, you may be big, but I'm much larger.

I follow him through the security door. My breathing gets heavier after the door slams closed behind me. I almost feel the walls caving in on me suffocating me again.

"Arms to the side, legs apart. I'm sure you know the drill." The guard pats me down looking for weapons. He isn't going to find any.

I stare at him hard. He flinches back for a second thinking I might hit him. Little does he know I have a good amount of self-control until it comes to Kylie. She seems to be the only person in the world who makes me lose it.

He brings me to the visitation area. Before he turns around, I look back at him and ask, "You have a wife at home?"

He looks at me not answering. My eyes go to his left hand finding a ring, bringing my eyes back up to his nervous ones, I grin. "I feel sorry that she never gets off because of your tiny dick. Maybe I'll go find her and show her how a real man fucks."

Turning my back to him, I lower myself into the chair. There is a glass window in front of me and a phone on my right. The prisoner comes walking in wearing an orange jumpsuit. The sound of the chains clanking on his ankles gets louder every step he takes in my direction. They connect up to the cuffs around his wrists. Absently, I rub my wrist reminding myself that I am free. Those chains no longer hold me prisoner, like they do him.

Not much has changed on him, appearance wise. His hair is longer now graying around the edges, but he's still a good-looking man. He also always looked exactly like him. Like Owen. Except for his eyes. His eyes are mine.

Reaching over he picks up the phone, "Ash."

"Dad."

"Been a long time, son." I follow his eyes to the guard burning holes through my body behind me. His face turns up into a smirk that matches my own. "I can see you haven't changed much."

"I've been busy." Shitty excuse but it's the only one I have. Ignoring his comment about the guard, I continue. "I see you didn't lack in a visitor," I finish coldly. I planned on keeping him out of this convo, but every time I see my father, Owen is the primary focus. Another reason I've stayed the hell away.

"Yeah, he tries to come here every month."

"I see that, and I don't give a fuck what he does." I snap at him, "He's been dead to me since he changed his name."

My father sighs looking defeated. I notice the wrinkles over his brows. Ones that I and my pig brother most likely put there. "You know he had to. Nothing good can be said about the last name Black. I dragged it through the mud, then you came along and buried it so deep it would take him saving a hundred children out of a burning school building, and that still wouldn't be enough to fix it. He's a police officer, Asher." I ball my fists on the table in front me. "He needed a clean reputation. One that isn't linked to me or you."

"He's a pussy. He's one of the people you raised me to hate!" My anger rises. This is why I've stayed away.

"He chose a different path than us. I was a fool. Look where I am now. Get it through your thick head, or you're going to end up in this exact seat talking to your son one day."

My heart stings when he mentions me with a son. I let that settle in. He can't possibly know how much that hits home.

"He loved her too, Ash," he tells me, and I scoff. He shakes his head at me. "Now you listen, and you listen well. I watched you, Owen, and Angelina growing up. I watched him chase her the minute he could pick up his big head and walk. I watched her too, and all she saw was you. But you, you didn't notice shit. You were exactly like me; you were too worried about partying and screwing girls. Not realizing you had that girls love your entire life and she had his. I knew one day when you were over yourself; you were going to notice her. I knew when that day came yours and your brother's relationship would be over. It happened, and it blew the hell up passed what I had even imagined. He lost more than you that day; he lost you, her, and a child."

"A child that was never supposed to be his!" I slam my fist down. Causing the guard to knock his nightstick against the wall. I glare at him from my seat, and he stops.

"Calm down. They made a mistake. You were locked up. She cried for you for months. She didn't want that life for you or her. The way you live is not something a woman wants for her husband. Am I saying what they did was right? Fuck no, Ash, but it happened, and now she's gone, and he's the only family you have out there in this world."

"Stop calling him my family. Your family doesn't bang your wife then hide that shit for months." My anger is boiling.

"Is that so? How about you tell me about the girl. Go ahead tell me you aren't dragging an innocent girl into your guys' shit." He glares at me.

I stop clenching my jaw; I hadn't even noticed I was doing it till now. "She's different."

"Yeah, Ash? He loves this one too. Been telling me about her for months. I know that's why you're here. She's gotten to you, and you're so screwed up in the head you don't know what to do."

He's right. He can read me like an open book. I'm without a doubt his son. Why did I come here? I rub my free hand over my face,

His hand tightens around the phone. "Leave her alone. Walk away. Don't let history repeat itself. Don't ruin her."

"I can't," I tell him, honestly.

"Shit," he curses, under his breath. "Goddamn it, Asher. What am I supposed to do here? I love you, son, and I love him too. I've made a ton of mistakes, but you two were the best things I've had in my life. I'm going to die in here one day, and I won't have any peace knowing my only two sons are out there tearing each other down over pussy."

"I won't let her go." I'm too selfish. I enjoy her in my house. I enjoy her more in my bed. There's no f way in hell I will let her walk out of my life and possibly back into his. I'm not the kind of man who will give up what I want. Not for her. Not for my father. Especially not for my asshole brother.

"Fine, then you better take care of her." He gives me one last look, then slams the phone down. He signals for the guard to take him back to his cell. I remain seated even after he's long gone.

My father is a hard man. His child life conditioned him for a life full of let downs and hardships. He grew up in a trailer park with a father who was a drunk and a mother who was a druggie. He did what he had to do to survive. Growing up, he wouldn't be winning any of the father of the year awards, but he did what he can to make sure Owen and I were always clothed and fed. He did what he had to for us. In all my life, I've never seen him look more defeated and upset than he did now, not even when the judge gave him life for murder.

I grew up to be exactly like him. He never wanted this life for me. If Kylie ends up knocked up by me, I vow never to let my child be like us or any of his uncles.

I pull off the highway into the parking lot of a dive bar on my way back to the hotel room. I'm prepared to drink my face off in alcohol. I want to forget this whole day happened. I want to numb out the sick feeling that's burrowed its way inside me since I landed in this humid as hell state.

Avoiding my father, avoiding the past has been my saving grace. Now it's like I was just thrown right back into it. Old thoughts about Angelina plague my mind. Knowing what everything my father said about Owen loving her was right. Thinking about how I might have chased her right into his arms. Now this whole mess with Kylie. It's too late now anyway. Wish I could say I regret dragging her into it, but I don't.

Shot after shot. Almost numb I keep going. Eventually, I stumble into the door of my hotel room. I hate my younger brother—Owen Black a.k.a. Officer Blake Owens. My last thoughts before I pass out, not even making it to the bed.

Chapter Twenty-Three

Kylie

Asher's been gone for four days, and I haven't heard a word since. I've gone through the stages starting from anger ending at upset. Now, I'm just at the point where I can't wait to go out with my girls tonight to let go. For once, I want to be a regular girl who doesn't live her life in the presence of dangerous men. If only for one night.

I hear the horn beep outside as I finish applying my red lipstick. I take a look in the mirror one last time at my outfit. I have on tight black leather pants paired with a black shirt that leaves the back completely open and dips in the front low enough to see a nice good amount of cleavage. On my feet are high red pumps. I'll most likely break an ankle out there, but they look hot, so it's a small price to pay. My long blonde hair is perfectly straight stopping just below my chest. My make-up is dark and smoky. I look like the type of woman that infamous Asher Black would have on his arm. I smile at my reflection knowing that he would blow his lid if he saw me leaving in this outfit without him here. It's perfect.

"Hey, girls," I greet my friends while getting settled in Steph's truck.

Taking me in she says, "You look smoking hot tonight."

"Thanks, you guys look awesome too!" They do. From what I can see, they are both rocking skin-tight dresses. Ashley's red dress leaves a lot of leg on display and little to the imagination. Steph's strapless black dress clings to her shape, leaving her large chest pouring over the top. They are going to be fighting off men left and right tonight. "Let's go get some drinks in us."

Club Silver is packed when we get there. The club has three different floors to it. Each level has a different color scheme and lighting. The music is blasting here, and bodies are moving in sync on the first floor. The lights are low leaving a sensual vibe. The second floor is more of a lounge. Couches are set up around the bar, which is a complete circle shape in the middle of the room. The second floor is for more intimate talking or just hanging with a group of friends. The third floor is where things get crazy. Some night they have foam machines running. Other nights they have paint machines that spray your body down in different colors as you're dancing. I love it here.

Chase and Tyler are saving a table for us in the VIP area. Chase gets hooked up every time he comes here. From what I've heard, he's won the owner a nice sum of money from his fights. Having Chase as a brother does have some pretty cool advantages, as well as having Tyler for a brother, too. My first car was plain, cute, and sporty when I bought it. Then Tyler came in and gave it a face-lift. The rims were turned pink, the lights were blue hid's, and the tinted windows were so dark you would think I was a famous person hiding from paparazzi. God, I love those two crazies.

The minute Chase sees Stephanie, he beelines for

her and wraps her up in his arms. She squeals as she tries to fight him away. Chase laughs at her attempts before throwing her over his shoulder and heading straight to the dance floor. Like a true caveman.

Ashley shakes her head. "Is he always like that with her?"

I laugh. "Yes, watch them tonight. He will throw his best lines at her. It's comical. I almost feel bad for the guy."

"Almost is the key word," Tyler chimes in, handing Ashley and I martinis.

I look to see where Chase is grinding against Steph on the dance floor, and I smile. I get what he sees in her. She's a tall blonde with a lean and athletic body but gifted with a chest that could make anyone envious. She's always dressed to kill. I don't think I've ever seen her without makeup perfectly on her face or a chip in her perfectly manicured nails. She comes from money, and it's obvious from looking at her. She isn't stuck up, though. She's everything Chase has never had, and that is the appeal. I fear one day she might give in to him. Then I'll most likely have to apologize to her and beg her to be my friend the next day still.

After watching Chase and Steph a little longer, I turn my focus to Tyler and Ashley, who are in deep conversation. Now those two would make sense, I think to myself.

"I'm going to head to the dance floor," I call to them, over the music.

"Okay, be careful," Tyler warns me with his eyes still focused on Ashley. I smile to myself, hoping maybe they hit it off.

Heading to the bar, I make my way to the dance

floor. Once I squeeze between two people, I order myself a shot of fireball and this time a vodka club. Martini's taste awesome, but tonight I need stronger. I need the type of drink that puts hair on your balls. Well if you had any, to begin with. After bringing the shot to my lips, I tip it back, then order another. I allow myself to get a nice buzz going before I'm feeling tipsy and ready to dance.

Once I'm on the dance floor, I'm lost to the world. My body moves to the beat of the music. A song in Spanish is playing, and I don't give a crap if I don't understand the lyrics, that melody is a hit.

My hands go up in the air and down my body while I sway my hips back and forth. The music flows through me making me come alive.

Arms wrap around me from behind, pulling me in close. One hand stops at my hip the other lay across my stomach. I feel a strong, warm chest behind me. Not as big as Asher's, but still tight and solid, and right now I don't care. I need a distraction, and this guy will have to do.

I turn my body around still wrapped in his arms and face him. Instantly, I tense up when I look up into a familiar pair of dark green eyes. Blake's eyes. A lump gets lodged in my throat.

He's looking down at my face. Taking me in and memorizing my features like it's the last time he's going to see me and hold me. Which most likely it is. My heart hurts from the guilt I feel inside. The look of heartbreak has taken over his handsome face, and that crushes me inside.

"Blake." I give him a soft smile.

He pulls me into him tighter. He feels warm and

comfortable. I don't feel the same thrill as I do when Asher holds me. I don't feel my body coming alive and excited like under Asher's touch. Asher sets me on fire just by his serious intense look. But right now, I do feel cherished and loved. I allow myself a few more seconds in his arms before pulling away.

"I can't." I break away from him, creating some distance between us.

He nods his head, understanding why I had to back away. "Come to the bar with me and at least talk to me." His eyes look sad and hurt, his hair grew in shaggier than usual, and even in the dark of the club, I can see the bags under his eyes.

I nod my head; I can at least give him that. He never did anything to hurt me. He was always sweet and respectful. Not harsh and demanding like Asher. They couldn't possibly be any more different, worlds apart really.

Placing his hand on my lower back, he ushers me to the bar. Here I won't have to scream over the music to talk to him. I order myself another drink since I'm going to need it.

"You look different," he tells me, then keeps going quickly, afraid he might have offended me. "Not in a bad way, just not like yourself."

I do look different. I feel different too. The girl that Blake dated was never the real me. He knew the lies I told him about my brothers and me. His idea of me being an innocent elementary school teacher couldn't be farther from the truth. Never once have I given off the impression that I go to clubs at nighttime, wearing skimpy clothing, gambling at poker tables. Most of the time he thought I was home and asleep. Finally, I have the freedom to be my old myself again. Asher knows me for who I am, no lies, no bullshit just the real me.

"This is me, Blake."

"Why, Kylie? Why are you with him? There is so much you don't know." He trails off stopping himself before saying more.

"What do you mean?" I ask him confused. "What do you know about him?"

"I've never lied to you before. I just need you to trust me. You have to stay away from him." His eyes are showing genuine concern for me, not at all jealousy.

"Why, Blake? You aren't making any sense."

He reaches for my hand and cups it in his. "Please. Just—"

"Remove your hand, Blake, before I remove it for you." A growl from a deep voice behind me startles me.

Blake drops my hand severing all connections and takes a step back, putting distance between us. I turn to see Asher stalking toward us with a look of murder in his eyes. I guess the devil is home, and holy crap does he look good with a tan. His blue eyes are practically glowing as they glare into Blake. A wave of emotion passes over me seeing him again. It's only been four days. Why do I feel like we've been apart for weeks?

Blake throws his hands up in surrender. "I was leaving," he states calmly and walks away. Asher continues to stare at him even after he's disappeared into a sea of people. The intensity in his eyes sends shivers up my spine.

"Asher," I call him, gently.

He turns around taking a step into my space. I back away on instinct, my back hitting the bar behind me. The anger hasn't left his beautiful face. His one lip is still curled up into a snarl making him look like an angry wolf ready to pounce.

"No," he hisses at me, "don't ever back away from me again." He pulls me in tight against his hard body, trapping me between him and the bar. I feel my body coming alive being close to him again. My skin breaks out in goosebumps, and I feel my nipples tightening in my bra. Goddamn him. I didn't realize how much I missed his touch till now.

Snapping out of my Asher-induced fog, I remember I'm still angry at him for leaving. I'm pissed at him for running away without telling me. I also still want him with everything inside me, and that angers me, too.

"Where are your clothes?" he growls at me while taking in my body from head to toe. "Out here dressed like this without me around! You trying to pick someone up?"

"Maybe I am." I push him away from him. He lets me go but not before grabbing my hand. He drags me through the crowd and toward the exit. I wobble in my heels trying to keep up with him, but his pace doesn't slow down. He stops pulling me once we get outside into the empty alleyway next to the club.

He throws my body against the building and presses his body close to mine, lowering his head till his breath fans my face. "Too bad for you no one touches you but me, and that goes for Blake. What were you doing with him? What did I tell you?" His body is tense, his jaw tight "Need to be taught another lesson? Is that it? Because baby, next time I'll fuck you in front of his face to prove my point."

I shoot him an angry glare. "Are you serious? You

left me without a word for days." I slam my fist into his chest. "And you come back here like a big bad tough guy, asking me what I'm doing! Well, fuck you, Asher!" I slam my hands against him harder this time.

His breathing is deeper. His nostrils flare. "Stop hititng me." His voice is demanding as he wraps his big hands around my tiny ones, holding them tight against his chest. His heart is pounding under our joined hands. Pulling and pushing, I try to free them. He's too strong and powerful for me. They don't budge from his tight grip.

"Why did he tell me to stay away from you? What is it between you two? Because I know something happened there." I'm tired of this game; someone needs to start talking. Asher glared at Blake as if he kicked his puppy or something. There is no way you can look at someone with that much hate in your eyes for no reason. Something huge happened between those two, and it's about time I know what.

Releasing my hands, he takes a step back, running his now free hand through his hair. "Shit!" He curses to himself, "Damn it!"

"No, you don't get to back away from me. You don't get to keep playing these mind games; I can't take it. I'm not doing this anymore." I'm yelling at him, not even bothering to control my temper anymore. I could give a shit less what he's capable of. He doesn't scare me, yet he terrifies me at the same time.

His blue eyes darken when they lock onto my green ones. His words are filled with so much anger. "The hell you aren't. You're mine, and I'm not letting you go anywhere." He stalks toward me again with a look of determination on his face. Closing in till he backs me up into the wall and his lips come crashing down on mine. I instantly wrap my arms around his neck and legs around his waist. I'm caged between his body and the wall. The feel of his solid abs beneath his shirt and muscled arms holding me up with ease sends my mind into a frenzy. I kiss him back with the fire inside of me.

I can feel his hard dick pressing against my core as he thrusts his hips up. "You make me crazy," he says, in between kissing me.

I'm lost in the world of Asher Black. Consumed by his chiseled body and talented tongue. His lips assault my neck while his hand fumbles with the button on my leather pants.

"I need to be in this wet pussy," he growls into my neck, freeing one of my legs from my pants, then grabs my crotch over my panties. He's going to have sex with me up against a wall outside of a club, and I don't care. Lost in the moment, there isn't anywhere else I want to be. As long as Asher is with me, nothing else matters. The need for him is stronger than any rational sense I have.

"Take me," I tell him, moaning heavy.

He frees his massive cock from his pants and rolls on a condom. He pushes my panties to the side not bothering to take them off; then he slams home. My head falls back, slamming into the wall behind me.

"God, yes!" I scream, as Asher's cock fills my body.

He drives into me hard, not letting up. Each thrust is with anger. His eyes are still narrow, burning into mine. My hands are clawing at his back and through his dark hair wildly. The stubble of his jaw rubs into my cheek. He laces his tattoo hand through mine, bringing both our hands up over my head, pressing them against the wall.

"This is mine. Kylie. You are mine," he tells me over and over, each time he slams into me.

"No, Asher. I don't belong to you." I do. In every way, I do.

He lets my hand go, then moves his hand wrapping it tightly around my throat. Showing me his control, showing me his possessiveness. "Yeah." His body thrust into me hard. "You." Again. "Do." Emphasizing every word making sure I'm paying attention, which I am. I hear and feel everything he is doing to me right now. He has that way of consuming me when his hard dick is inside me.

"Asher!" I scream breathless as my orgasm whips threw me at the same time I feel him pulsing inside me.

He drops his forehead to mine resting on me. Our breathing is frantic. He places a small peck on my lips.

"Yeah you do," he says, again calmly.

"I do," I whisper back.

Chapter Twenty-Four

Asher

"Do you see him?" Jimmy asks, from the passenger seat of our unmarked car.

"No." I lower my baseball cap to cover my eyes. I can't allow him to see me. If he does, he will run like the pussy he is.

We've been staked out for two hours waiting for Logan to show up. My anger is increasing the more time passes. My mind is running on different scenarios on how I'm going to end his shitty life. The longer he takes, the more creative I become.

He's been like a thorn in my side for weeks now, went underground since the attack on Kylie. All that did was buy him some time. He's smart enough to know I'm coming for him. By no means is he a genius for fucking with me in the first place. If he were, he would be trading in his Chicago Bears hat for a drink on a beach somewhere in Mexico.

The shit Logan pulled with Kylie has had me on edge. On top of that, catching Owen at the club talking to her was enough to send me over. When I left, I had people watching her. That's how I knew she went out to the club that night in the first place. Jimmy texted me the second I landed. Didn't tell her that shit, though, she'd throw her attitude at me had she known she was being followed. There was no possible way I would have left her alone, unprotected. I can't keep her locked in my house as much as I want to. Although, the thought of her chained to my bed makes my cock harden.

Jimmy chugs the rest of his coffee before throwing the empty cup to the ground. He looks as exhausted as I feel. "You think he'll show tonight?"

Yes, tonight he will show up at the old sports bar we are parked across the street from. The Stone Inn has been around since I was a kid. My father would take Owen and me here every Sunday during football season. If he won his bets that day, we would get treated like kings with steak dinners. If he lost, we were lucky to have bread and water.

The place is old but by no means outdated. Inside there are flat screen TV's hanging on every wall. Every possible sports game is played on them. It's a gambler's wet dream. Logan comes here every few weeks to pay his bookie and place new bets. Little does he know that his bookie owes me one.

"Yeah, Stone called in his favor earlier. Told me he owes him a hefty sum. If he doesn't show, he'll have more than me to worry about." I wouldn't take that threat lightly. I don't mind his boys knocking him around a bit, but I want him alive. He knows this.

Andrew Stone is a man you don't want to piss off. I've seen him do shit that makes me look like a saint. I wouldn't go as far as calling us friends. For now, we stay out of each other's way. It won't be long before one of us has to take the other out. I'd be stupid if I didn't see him as a considerable threat.

His son landed himself in some trouble with a local MC a few years back. He was found fooling around with one of the member's old lady. Everyone knows if you screw around with a member's old lady, you better prepare yourself for an early grave. Stone made a call asking me for help. A man like him doesn't ask anyone for help. He has too much pride, which shows how desperate he was and how thick of shit he was currently in. He's getting older and by no means was ready for a full-blown war. He knew the MC wouldn't fuck with the relationship they have with me. I keep the cops off their asses while they run guns through the city. Lucky for him the member whose wife it was had been caught stealing from the club. Long story short, they handed Stone's son over to me, and I let him go. Since then he's been indebted to me. I knew one day it would come into use. Keep your friends close and enemies closer.

A black pick-up truck pulls in the lot to the right of the bar. I recognize it immediately. Three men get out and file inside. I can tell one of the men is Logan. Between his arrogant prick strut and his hoodie, I knew it was him. He should have burnt every hoodie he owned. Dead giveaway. That's the problem with him. He seems to think he's untouchable.

"Bingo," I say to Jimmy, who's checking his gun for ammo. I pull my own from the glove box, only loading one bullet in the chamber. I only ever have one in the chamber. If I'm firing my gun, I'm shooting to kill. One clean shot. I tuck it into the back of my jeans.

Jimmy rolls his eyes at me. "You're a cocky shit you know that?"

The corner of my lip raises into a smirk. "I'm confident."

We head to the back of the building. The door

under the fire escape leads to the back rooms. This is where degenerates come in, throwing down vast wads of cash with hopes and dreams that their teams are going to win. Shit, I've seen bets made on the coin toss during the Super Bowl. This whole operation is a gold mine. Being a bookie was never something I got involved with, though. I prefer to stick to what I know; decks of cards and green cloth tables.

I walk inside and am met with two guards blocking the way. The men are huge, armed, and ready. I pull off my baseball hat and throw it to the side. Won't be needing it anymore. Logan's going to get a good look at the man who's about to end him. The guards take a look at my face, nod, and back out of my way. They knew I would be coming. Had they not we would have been shot on the spot. Questions asked later.

Slowly, we make our way down the hall. The last door is cracked enough for me to see inside. Stone is sitting at a large desk talking to Logan whose back is toward us. Stone's eyes lock into mine a slight nod of his head tells me we are even. I quietly slip inside. My breathing is steady. I enjoy the surprise factor. Call me dramatic, but I prefer to stalk like a lion before jumping in for the kill.

"I don't have your money this week," Logan tells him with a hint of fear in his voice. "I've been on lockdown since Asher put the word out to find me. I need another week."

"You don't have another week." Stone smiles at him, nodding toward me in the shadows. His smile is anything but friendly. It sends chills up my spine, and I'm a hard motherfucker.

Taking a step out of the dark, Logan turns to face

me. Shock registers first before his face goes white and he backs away. With nowhere to go and nowhere to hide.

"You set me up!" he screams at Stone, who laughs like the crazed man he is.

I take out my gun, putting the silencer on and raising it. He's still as I watch piss stream down his pants. Pathetic. At least he doesn't beg for his life like his brother. He knows he's about to die. My face will be the last thing he will ever see. He should be happy it's a handsome face.

I pull the trigger, landing a bullet straight between his eyes. Blood sprays the wall behind him as his body falls with a loud thump. His dead eyes remain open on the ground. I wait for a feeling of guilt to set in, but nothing comes as I tuck my pistol back into my jeans. "Oh, it was me who killed your piece of shit brother, by the way." I tell the dead body at my feet.

Stone doesn't flinch at the sight of him either. His eyes are cold. Can't say I look any different right now. Killing a person is like waking up and drinking a cup of coffee to men like us. He doesn't even pay mind to the blood covering his wall or the fact a dead body is lying in his office. Sick fuck.

"Black." he finally greets me.

"Stone," I reply taking him in, noticing his once salt and pepper hair has now turned entirely white. There are more wrinkles around his dark eyes and mouth, as he puffs his cigar. I try to think of how old he is now, but I can't. He's one of those people who has looked old since I was a kid, then I grew up and here I am wondering how the hell he is still living and still looking old as dirt.

He takes a puff of his cigar, smoke pours from his mouth and his nostrils as he speaks, "This makes us even."

"Yes." I nod hating the fact he ever owed me one, to begin with.

"She worth all this?" He raises a white eyebrow.

The problem with that is I never told him why I was after Logan. The question doesn't sit right with me. He knows she could be my weakness. One that could be used against me in the future.

"She's nothing to me, but revenge." I keep a straight face. I've been trying to convince myself that since day one. No clue why it sounds foreign coming out of my mouth.

Stone lets out another evil laugh. "Heard she's a gorgeous little thing, good at poker too."

"Not good enough. How do you think she landed in my possession to begin with?"

"I already know the details. I'd like to meet her one day."

Over my dead body. "She won't be around long enough." Another lie.

"We'll see. Goodbye, Black."

"Later, Stone."

I walk out knowing that was one less problem, yet somehow it appears that another one might have just taken its place. The story of my life.

Chapter Twenty-Five

Kylie

I'm woken from a deep sleep by the sound of frantic pounding on the front door. I shoot up fast feeling my heart racing out of my chest. Even in the pitch black, I'm aware that Asher still isn't in for the night. His presence is comparable to a winter coat wrapped around me. His eyes are blanketing me, heating me up even when he's at a distance. I'm finally coming to terms with my awareness of him. I catch myself searching around for him when he enters a room. When I do spot him, he becomes my only focus making everyone around him non-existent.

Going to the nightstand next to the bed, I grab the gun that Asher keeps there. There are guns hidden in every corner of this house. Since our little makeup outside the club a few weeks ago, things have gotten better. He now trusts me enough not to kill him in his sleep. With that came the knowledge of the location of his weapons. His house is comparable to that of Mr. and Mrs. Smith. If ever there was an apocalypse, I know exactly where to go. It's to the point where he even hides a gun next to the toilet bowl. I hope that is one I never have to use.

Crawling around to the front of the house, I pop my head out to peek out the window. Shaking my head when I realize I'm not by any means a ninja, I walk to the door. If someone were here to kill me, they wouldn't be announcing their presence. Whoever is out there is practically waking up the whole neighborhood. Opening the door still holding the gun in my hand in case, I'm pushed aside by Chase who frantically storms passed me, letting himself into every room opening and closing all the doors.

"Jesus, Chase, what the hell?" I ask, surprised to see him.

"Black home?" He questions me while turning around taking me in. His eyes look down to the gun in my hand. "And what did you plan on doing with that?"

"No, he's still out, and I planned on using it if need be."

Chase rolls his eyes now making his way into the kitchen. He takes in Asher's house looking around. He looks as if he is searching for something. I wonder what the hell it is.

"Chase, seriously what is going on?" I ask again.

He pauses in front of me putting his hands on my shoulders. "Go pack your shit. You're leaving with me."

"No, I'm—" I begin to tell him.

"Logan is dead," he cuts me off before I finish my sentence.

My eyes widen in shock. I'm speechless as Chase continues, "Happened a few hours ago..." he pauses looking around again, taking his hands off my shoulders, he throws them in the air. "And as you can see Asher isn't home, so it would appear that..."

"How the hell do you know this already? Do you guys have a criminal hotline or something that you all report back to?" A nervous laugh slips out before I can catch it.

Chase shrugs finding no humor at my nervous joke. "People talk on the streets. Asher's smart. If he didn't want anyone to know, then they wouldn't. Clearly, he wanted a message sent out regarding you. Which is why you are leaving with me."

"Chase, I can't just leave. I made a deal with him. He won't let me go anyway. He'll be breaking our door down by morning." I assure myself even though I'm not too confident in that statement. Truth is I don't want to leave him. I feel so much for the man. I know he isn't a good man. I know he kills without any remorse, but those hands he uses to kill he also uses to be gentle with me. Problem is he never told me I was more to him than just a warm body, and that weighs on my heart.

"Kylie, this is the second man he has killed for you. Snap the hell out of it. He's dangerous. Let him try to take you back. He can take that up with Tyler and me."

I feel my eyes tearing up. Chase is right. How can I love someone who can take another life like its nothing? At the moment I'm forced to leave him, I realize I love him. I don't even know when or how that happened, but I know in my heart that I do. More than my heart, I feel it with everything inside me. Chase pulls me into his chest and lets me cry into him. I'm shocked at this side of him I never knew existed. It's a welcomed change.

I let Chase talk me into leaving Asher. He waits downstairs while I pack my things from our bedroom. Tears pour down my face, soaking into his shirt that I was wearing to sleep tonight. Asher loves it when I sleep in one of his shirts. Just yesterday I was making us breakfast when he came downstairs to find me in his ratty old Nirvana tee. He lifted me onto the counter, parted my thighs, and dove in like I was the only breakfast he needed.

I strangle down a sob thinking about how close we've come in the last few weeks. I noticed him slowly coming home earlier at night. He would eat dinner with me and ask me how my day was. He even went as far as helping me grade papers for my students. Well, he more laughed at some of the ridiculous answers the children gave, but things felt simple and ordinary. The sex had been fantastic too. Ever since that night, we haven't been able to keep our hands off each other.

My heart is torn into two pieces. One half is in love with the gentle, caring man he can be, and the other half is terrified of the monster that hides within him. I struggle to wonder what kind of person it makes me to be in love with a beast.

"Come on, Kylie," Chase yells from downstairs growing impatient, pulling me from my thoughts.

I gather as much stuff that I can fit into a bag. We have to hurry. I know we have to get out of here before Asher comes home, and I'll be forced to watch him and my brother kill each other. Chase is waiting at the bottom of the stairs for me. I walk down confidently as if I'm not leaving my heart behind. We hop into Chase's pick-up truck and head home.

My heart breaks the farther away we drive.

Chapter Twenty-Six

Kylie

I've woken again from the feel of light kisses up my neck and down my jawline. My pulse quickens, Asher's breath is warm on my face, and the smell of his cologne wraps around me, consuming me. The scent of him instantly comforts me when it should do nothing more than terrify me.

I pretend to remain asleep. Trying to calm my breathing, I keep my eyes tightly shut. I'm not ready for this. He's going to be furious with me.

Bending over my body, blocking the little bit of light that was creeping into my room, Asher whispers in my ear, "I know you're awake. Your heart is racing."

His voice is calm and cold. His broad body casts a shadow over me as I rub my now open eyes. His face is inches from mine, but it's so dark in my room that all I can make out are the sky color of his eyes. Asher runs his fingers lightly down the side of my face, down to my neck, and across my collarbone.

"I wasn't—" as soon as the lie leaves my lips his fingers dig harder into the flesh of my neck. I'm pushing his patience. I swallow nervously. "How did you get in here?"

I know for sure I locked the door and all the windows of the house to prevent this exact thing from happening. Even in the dark, I can tell he has a smug smirk on his face. Be proud of the fact you can perform a B & E so well; I'm about to say, as it sits on the tip of my tongue, but I stop myself before it comes out.

"Want to tell me why you aren't you in my house? Asleep in my bed? I don't remember telling you that you were free to leave, yet." His voice is still eerily calm, and steady.

"Want to tell me what happened to Logan Lloyd?" I challenge back.

"Fucking Chase," Asher says under his breath, shaking his head. "So that's what this is about?" He leaves the bed and stands in the middle of my room, crossing his arms. He looks like a giant in my tiny bedroom.

Sitting up in bed, I can finally see him. I lean against my cushioned headboard taking in his beautiful face. He has bags under his eyes, and he looks exhausted. I notice he's wearing a black tee and jeans that aren't zipped up. His shoe ties remain open, and his wet hair is disheveled. This is the first time I've ever seen him not look perfectly groomed. Instead, he seems as if he only stopped home to shower and throw clothes on before coming to find me. And even though he came right to me after killing someone, I can still feel the love I have for him pouring out around me.

"Asher." I try to keep the tears from spilling down my face. I've cried so much tonight I'm not even sure how I have any left in me. "You have no idea what this is doing to me. I can't be okay with the fact that I'm in love with someone who can take a life like it's nothing."

Asher stalks back over to me. Climbing onto the bed, he puts his hands on each side of my face holding himself up. "What did you say?" His voice cold.

I push from him backing up farther into the headboard. I wish the bed would swallow me whole. "That I can't be with someone who kills?" I answer back, knowing that isn't what he wants me to repeat.

"Kylie, stop screwing around and repeat it."

So, I say it. Tears are streaming down my face with Asher hovering over me. I tell Asher Black the handsome hard man that I love him.

He looks down at me like he's angry. He looks at me like I thoroughly pissed him off with my love. He doesn't say it back. I don't see any love in his hard eyes either. He says nothing at all and walks out my door. In a real Asher Black fashion.

My hands go to my chest to soothe the hurt from where Asher just ripped my heart out.

Chapter Twenty-Seven

Asher

She loves me. She fucking loves me. That was not part of the plan. I wanted her trust. Maybe even her baby, but her love? No, that was not something I ever wanted again. It's been years since the last time I've heard those dreadful three words.

"I love you," Angelina says, standing in front of me pregnant with a baby that was never mine, her big brown eyes are sad, they used to be vibrant and full of so much life. She looks worn down still beautiful, but her eyes don't shine with the same happiness they did before I went in. Before she made the mistake that lost me before I hated her with everything inside me. Somehow, I still loved her.

"Get out of my house," I yell at her. It's been a few hours since I found out Owen my brother. My best friend. My flesh and blood is the father. I've been too stunned to move from the spot I've been sitting in and I'm at a loss of words. I've only been out of jail for a little over a month, and this is the shit I came home to.

Her tiny body is shaking. Tears streak her face. Her lips are trembling. I want nothing more than to wrap her in my arms and tell her it's going to be okay. I was never able to watch her cry, even when we were kids. I don't do it though. I don't touch her.

"Please Ash, I'm sorry, I'm so sorry," she pleads

with me, in between sobs.

I feel numb. My brother and my wife. Together screwing while I was in jail. I asked him to look out for her while I was away. I sure as shit wasn't expecting this. And a baby. Shit.

She walks over to me and bends down in between my legs resting her forehead on my chest. She wraps her arms around me tightly. I let her stay like that and cry into me. I don't say any kind words to soothe her or rub my hands down her back as I used to when she was upset. I'm dead on the inside, but I let her have these last few minutes holding me.

Eventually, I get up and unwrap myself from her arms. "Pack your bags tonight. Go to Blake's. The baby deserves his family." I walk out leaving her hysterical in the middle of what used to be our home.

I didn't know that was the last night I would ever see her alive.

Ever since that day, I swore off ever loving another person again. It's been so long I'm not even confident I'm capable of that emotion anymore. I'm not entirely heartless. I feel possessive over Kylie. I care about her and would kill for her as I have twice already. She gives me a spark that I thought has been long burned out for a long time. But love? No.

I'll give her space now to get over this love shit. Our lives are not a Nicholas Sparks novel. There won't be a fairytale happy ending here. She could be pregnant right now with my baby for all she knows, and if she is, we aren't going to be some happy little family. I will, without a doubt, take care of my kid. I will see that they both have everything they need, and they will always be protected. But I will never get married again. There will never be a minivan parked in our driveway with a white picket fence while I am out working a nine to five in an office with a fat, balding boss who has a permanent coffee stain on all of his dress shirts. No way.

She may hate the life I live and the darkness that lives inside me, but this is all I know. She's going to have to accept that because I won't let her leave me. Even if she isn't pregnant, I will fix that problem eventually. Once she finds out what I've done and who Blake is to me, I can be positive that love is not what she will be feeling for me. She'll be better off that way, and I will see that we keep a relationship based on mutual respect, never love. She will be safe, spoiled, and well fucked. That's all I can offer her, and I won't give her a choice to refuse.

There's just one last part of the puzzle that needs handling. There's no way in hell I'm going to fight her asshole brothers for the rest of my life. Time to put it to rest. Taking out my phone, I flip to Chase's name. He picks up on the first ring.

"Black."

"Tank." The name greet is the way we do it in our world. I am expecting nothing different. No warm hello or how was your day? It's always the same. We aren't friends, but we respect one another. For now.

"What do I owe the pleasure?" Chase asks, sarcastically.

"Saturday night, me and you in The Pit." He may be undefeated, but I have years of experience over the boy. After Angelina died, I fought nonstop. I didn't give a shit if I lived or died at that point. I was at a place where I had nothing to live for anymore. It drove me to become a machine. I went out undefeated, so this should be a hell of a fight.

Chase laughs. "Why?"

"Kylie." He knows what this is about. He wants to hear me say it out loud. "I knock you out, then you stay the hell out of our lives. She comes with me, and it's for good this time."

"You want me to fight you for my sister?"

"No, I want you to stay out of our lives and mind your own goddamn business. If you're not confident you can beat me, then that's another story." I'm baiting him. He's a hot head. I know what to say to him to get my things my way. I always know how to manipulate people.

"You're an asshole; she's too good for you."

"I know, but I don't give a shit. I'll see you Saturday. Keep Kylie away and don't tell her shit about this." I snap the phone shut. I know he'll be there. Men like Chase won't back down from a fight. He has way too much pride. If not, then he knows he's a pussy, and I won.

Chapter Twenty-Eight

Asher

I walk into the Pit on Saturday night. The crowds have been insane for every one of Chase's fights. Once word got out that Asher "Monster" Black and Chase "Tank" Turner were going to fight, the neighborhood exploded. I roll my eyes at the name "Monster." It was given to me by the crowd. Guess it could be worse.

"Asher, baby." Some blonde chick steps in front of me putting her hand on my chest. I push her off me. She frowns pouting out her injected lips that make her look like a fish. She's not Kylie. Nowhere in the same league as her. Her make up is plastered so thick on her face that she'll need a chisel to get it off later. I haven't had the slightest bit of interest in any girl since Kylie walked into my club. Kylie has natural beauty. She's soft and innocent with a wild ass temper that gets my dick hard.

Heading back to the back locker rooms with my bag in my hand, I'm focused on tonight's fight. I pop my headphones in my ear blasting heavy metal to get the blood pumping through my veins. I wrap my hands up in white tape. They stay steady as I feel the adrenaline coursing through my body. It's compared to the rush I get when I pull the trigger of my gun. The moments before I'm about to take someone's life.

I haven't fought in years. I've missed the thrill of

this. The past week I've spent in the boxing ring at the gym, preparing for this fight. Letting Jimmy handle all this side shit, so I remained focused. Not having nearly enough time to prepare adequately, but I want this win so bad. For once, I'm fighting with a purpose. I will not lose tonight.

The door swings open pulling me from my thoughts. Tyler walks in then leans up against the blue painted lockers, quietly. He doesn't say anything noticing the earbuds in my ear. The worst thing in the world is when you have earbuds in and people try to talk to you. When the song finishes I pull them out and give him my attention.

"Kylie here tonight?" I ask him.

"No," he replies, "she has been held up in her room all week, barely even comes out to eat. I take it you're responsible for that?"

My cold heart stings slightly at the thought of her upset over me, but I keep my face impassive. Tyler doesn't need to know his sister has me, as much as I have her.

"You can blame Chase for that," I deadpan. Yea, I pulled the trigger, but I didn't drop the bomb.

Tyler looks at me raising his eyebrow. "Whatever helps you sleep at night."

"What are you doing in here anyway?" I ask annoyed at his presence.

"Don't fight him," he says with a straight face. I begin to interrupt. He puts up his hands up, stopping me. "You have nothing to prove. This is ridiculous. If Kylie finds out, she's going to lose it."

"And I take it you just came back from having this talk with him?" He looks around the room avoiding me.

I notice his eye is slightly swollen. I focus on it smirking, "How'd that go for you?"

"Exactly how you think it went. I didn't give myself this black eye. Between the two of you violent shits, I'm going to be blind, toothless, and unable to have kids."

He starts laughing when he finishes. I can't help but smile back. "I hate to admit this, but I like you. I'm still fighting your thickheaded brother, though. I need him to back off, and I hope you will too after tonight."

Tyler sighs. "I hate to admit this even more because you're probably putting your filthy hands on my little sister." I shoot him a grin. Yeah, I'm screwing her, owning that shit too. He shakes his head at me. "But I respect you, and I know you will keep her safe. After watching her this week, I've never seen her like this. I can admit she needs you. Just don't kill him tonight."

"I sure as hell want to," I say under my breath. The sound of Tyler's laugh echoes down the hall after his retreating frame. I shake my head and finish wrapping my hands. I grab my Gatorade bottle as Jimmy walks through the door, telling me I'm up.

My adrenaline is pumping through my veins. It's time.

Chapter Twenty-Nine

Kylie

"Leave me alone, Tyler," I say into my cell phone that has been ringing not stop for the last hour. You would think he would get the hint that I don't want to talk from the previous fifteen calls I've ignored.

It's not him; personally, I don't want to talk to anyone right now. I want to resume lying in my bed curled up in a ball for the rest of my life. I've been this way since Asher walked out of my door and out of my life a few nights ago. To say he broke my heart would be an understatement. He shattered me and left me in tiny pieces of my former self.

"Kylie, don't hang up." The desperate tone of his voice has me sitting up. A slight wave of nausea hits me from getting up too quickly. I sit still taking in deep breathes, calming myself down. I swallow the feeling.

"What's going on?"

"I, uh, I'm at The Pit. Need your help with Chase."

"Okay, I'm coming."

Scrambling around my room, I pick up clothes off the floor; I haven't done any laundry. I've barely even gotten out of bed to shower so I can imagine I smell ripe right now. The worst part of that is, I genuinely don't care. I don't care about anything anymore. I'm completely numb.

I wasn't even aware that Chase fought tonight. I've

been a horrible sister to them for days. Chase came in trying to get me out of bed yesterday. I threw the remote at his head. Missed him and watched it shatter into pieces against the wall. He left me alone after that one.

A taxi drops me off into the parking lot of the abandoned building. I pay the man my fare, then head inside the Pit. Shivers run up my spine once I'm in the door and look around. The place is empty, besides the beer cans and cigarette butts that litter the floor. My footsteps echoing off walls is the only noise in the entire building. The crowds must have filed out hours ago, leaving the place deserted.

"Tyler?" I call out, my voice bouncing off the concrete. I continue searching the empty building. I follow the only light I can see and wind up in the old locker room. The paint chips off the walls, and it smells like dirty gym socks.

"Kylie, over here." Tyler's voice calms me from my nervousness.

I turn the corner toward the showers; my jaw drops once inside. Chase is laying on the ground entirely still. The top half of his body is covered in bandages that wrap from his left shoulder, across his ribs, and around his waist. Purplish bruises mark up his left, and his right eye is swollen shut. He looks as if he were struck by a car, then the car backed up over him again.

Tyler is sitting in a chair to his right, holding a bag of ice to Chase's head in one hand and the other is his cell phone. From the music coming from his phone, I can hear that he's casually playing clash of clans as if our brother isn't half-dead beside him.

"He got knocked out tonight, hell of a fight. He

woke up for a few minutes to take pain pills then passed out again and has been this way since. I've slapped him, poured a bucket of water on him, even got some girl in here trying to wake him up, and nothing." Throwing his arms up he continues, "I thought for sure the girl would have worked. That's how we know it's bad."

I rush to Chase's side, dropping down to my knees. "Oh my god. Shouldwetakehim to the hospital? Isheokay?" I shoot questions out fast, making them sound like one long ramble rather than actual English.

"Calm down. He's fine. Doctor Joe came in and looked at him. He may have a concussion, though. Honestly, this is good for him. Now, maybe he won't be such a cocky asshole." He puts down his cell phone, finally giving me his attention.

I calm down a little. "I still think we should take him to the hospital."

Tyler shakes his head. "And tell them what? Yes, Doctor, he was participating in an illegal fighting ring. Doctor Joe is fine."

"Who the hell would trust a doctor that goes by his first name?" That sounds comparable to a back-alley tattoo artist.

Tyler laughs. "Don't be ridiculous Kye. He's not a real doctor." Rolling his eyes at me, he continues, "Now help me get him into the car."

I'm too shocked and physically drained to even argue with him at this point. I shuffle around Chase's colossal frame to try to pick up his legs. Before I'm able to pick him up a thought occurs to me. I freeze. No, no, no.

"Kylie?" Tyler lets Chase's arm drop and turns toward me, noticing something is off.

"Who?"

"Kylie," he says again, this time softly.

I look up, staring him straight in the eyes, "Tyler I know only one man capable of this. Tell me it is not who I am thinking."

He looks away from me, "You already know who did this."

"Say it." In demand, I need to know for sure.

"Asher."

A pained sob groan escaped my lips, "Why? I don't understand. Tyler, he left me."

Tyler looks at me with sadness in his eyes. He hates seeing me upset. Ever since I was little, he was the one who would hold me when I cried and read me stories when I was sick. "I don't know, sis, you have to ask him yourself," he finishes, with a small smile.

Pushing the questions to the back of my head, for now, I bring my attention back to the task at hand. Thinking about how we are supposed to move over two hundred fifty pounds of solid muscle.

Chapter Thirty

Asher

By morning, my head is throbbing. Reaching over the nightstand, I grab the bottle of painkillers and pop the top open. I swallow three down without any water because I'm convinced I'm going to need a crane to lift myself out of bed. I choke them down. Knocking Chase out last night didn't come without a whole world of pain, but not having to deal with his shit for the rest of my life was well worth it.

By the time I'm able to pull myself out of bed, it's almost noon. My stomach is turning from hunger, and my body feels as if it's been trampled by a herd of elephants. I make it down the steps noticing a cop car pull up my driveway through the window.

"Last freaking thing I was in the mood for, "I mumble to no one.

On my way to the kitchen, I swing open the front door inviting the asshole in before he's out of his car. The sound of the door shutting and his footsteps down the hall make my anger grow. Ignoring it, I continue searching for something to eat. The tension in my kitchen is as thick as it always is whenever we are in the same room. Or same state, for that matter.

"What do you possibly want, Owen?" I speak first not once looking in his direction.

"You win," he says.

"Win what? Get to the point or get the fuck out," I snap at him.

"You know what. This game you're playing. You got Kylie; you rubbed it in my face. We are even. Please just leave her alone now."

"No."

"Damn it, Asher!" He runs his hand through his hair, a habit he's done for as long as I can remember when he's frustrated. "I'm sorry. I don't know how many times I can tell you that. I loved her, and you know it. We made a mistake. One mistake that cost me not only my brother, but the love of my life, and my baby and here I am years later still punished for it."

Finally, I pull my attention up from the sandwich I made and look at him. I notice the bags under his eyes first. Then take in the wrinkled uniform he has on. Staring back at me is a troubled man who looks like he hasn't gotten any sleep in weeks. He feels how I look right now. I can't deny anymore what has been in front of me for years. "I know you loved her."

"I love Kylie too. Please, Asher let her go. You know it is best for her she doesn't deserve any of this. She deserves better than the both of us."

He's right, but I don't care. "No," I tell him again.

Slamming his fist on the counter, he looks at me in disgust. "What is your plan here, Asher? Huh? Are you going to sleep with her? Maybe put a baby into her to really make us even? Is that what you want?"

I don't respond. I have nothing to say considering that was my plan. He doesn't remove his eyes from my face. He's watching my body language and expression reading my every move. Owen is an asshole, but he's always been good at reading people, except for Kylie, which has helped him advance in his shitty career.

"No, no." He shakes his head in horror. "What did you do? Please tell me you didn't."

"Kylie, you can come out now." I keep my back to her.

A small gasp comes out of her lips as she appears from behind me. Owen's face shows shock, but only long enough for me to catch it. He was unaware she was here listening to every word. I, on the other hand, was aware of her the second she showed up a few minutes after Owen walked in.

"Kylie," Owen calls to her softly, taking a step in her direction. "Please, let me explain."

I stand up quickly, knocking the chair down as I walk into his path, putting my body between hers and his. No way am I letting him go to her. A sob that escapes from her that has me turning around. She backs away from me instantly. Tears are pouring from her green eyes. Her face is paper white as one of her hands covers her stomach.

"I-I can't b-be, can I?" she whispers to herself. I take a step forward before she lashes out at me.

"*Get away from me!*" she screams, then runs past me grabbing the keys to my truck on her way out the door.

Owen chases after her screaming her name, but he's too late. All that's left is the sight of my taillights, already retreating down the street. He looks up to the porch at me from his patrol car.

"History repeating itself. I hope you're happy. If anything happens to her, this time it's on you." He gets into his car, slams the door, and speeds away.

Chapter Thirty-One

Kylie

The happy face on the pregnancy test I just took stares back at me, mocking me. I'm pregnant with Asher Black's baby. I've been staring at the stick for minutes, or maybe hours, hoping it would magically change.

When I went to his house earlier today, I was planning on giving him hell for his fight with Chase. What I didn't expect was to see the patrol car sitting in his driveway. I tried letting myself into the back door thinking it would go unnoticed. I should have known he would know I was there the whole time. Even with his back toward me. He knew what he was doing. He wanted me to hear everything. I did.

Blake is his brother, lifting up the toilet bowl lid I lose my lunch inside. My ex-boyfriend is going to be the uncle of my child. The child that I had no idea was growing inside me. A child that Asher made with me as a big fuck you to his brother who knocked up his wife. I was nothing more than a pawn in a game.

Wiping my mouth with my free hand, I place the positive pregnancy test on my bathroom sink. Then I lose it. Gripping onto the shower curtain, I pull it to the ground cursing, knocking all my shampoo bottles to the ground with it. I launch a candle into the mirror hanging above the sink, shattering into a million pieces.

171

Fifteen years of lousy luck sounds like child's play compared to the fact I'm now stuck with Asher for the next eighteen. I don't stop my meltdown till it looks like a tornado came through destroying everything in its path. Just like Asher does to everything he touches. I let out all the anger until there's nothing left and I'm sinking into the cold hard floor with sobs rocking my body uncontrollably.

The door opens up, and a blank-faced Asher steps inside. He takes in the scene around him, then his cold eyes land on me. He stares for a second before walking over to the sink and picking up the pregnancy test. I watch him for any sign of emotion, but nothing comes as he looks at it then sets it back down.

Before I can react, he picks me up and has me in his strong arms pressed against his chest. Walking me out of the bathroom, we pass a pissed off Chase and Tyler on the way to my bedroom. I brace myself for the fight that's about to happen, silently hoping they throw Asher out on his ass. Then nothing. Nothing happens as they move out of his way and let us pass as another whimper escapes my lips.

My body starts to sink as he places me down in the center of my bedroom. His arm quickly shoots out wrapping around me, holding me up. Steadying me because physical exhaustion has taken me over. My energy is spent. I have nothing left inside of me to argue or fight as he begins stripping me out of my clothes. He picks me up again and sets me on my bed in nothing but my bra and panties. I lie down and curl into a ball on my comforter, keeping my back toward him. I can hear the sound of his zipper as he undresses.

I let out a small sob when I feel his hard body

wrapping around me. My back is to his front. He pulls me in till there isn't an inch of space left between us. He gently wraps his arm around me, placing his outstretched hand protectively over my stomach. Over our baby. More sobs rock through me. Finally, when I'm able to get out a question, I ask him something I've been wondering.

"What were the cards in your hand that night?" Did he even win that day? Was this his plan from the beginning?

Even from behind me, I can feel his cruel smile growing. "The King and Queen of Spades."

T.A. Torres

About the Author

I live in a small town in New Jersey with my fiancé and our two crazy puppies. I'm an x-ray technician who spends every free minute of my day typing away writing fiction on my phone. You will rarely ever find me without a book in one hand and coffee in the other. I'm a firm believer that you can never get too much sleep, and I love antiques, gardening, crocheting, and my Vespa.

~*~

Visit T.A. at
https://m.facebook.com/tinaangelawrites

~*~

To chat with T.A. Torres and other Wild Rose Press authors of erotic romance, join us at
www.groups.yahoo.com/group/thewilderroses.

Play a Game with Me
Games People Play Book One
By Cadence Vonn

Maximilian Westfield has resurrected his family's company under the controlling eye of the major shareholder—his mother. To keep the company, he must marry the woman she chooses, no matter how inane or spineless. He is resigned to go through with the arranged marriage until he meets a feisty costume designer who will never meet his mother's standards. A stolen kiss spurs his lustful cravings. Once he tastes the spirited beauty's charms, he knows he has to find a way to keep her and his company. No other woman will do.

The daughter of a powerful British businessman, Teresa Medici Staffordshire leads her life as Tess Medici to avoid men out to please her father. Then she meets Maximilian, a sexy uptight CEO. From the moment he unleashes his expert fingers on her skin, she's hooked. His erotic games make her body hum with pleasure. Determined to lure Max out to play, every encounter becomes a game of enticement. But his commitment to his family business and his mother's determination to marry him off makes it impossible to take the relationship public, and Tess refuses to be his guilty little secret.

Choices become consequences, their future is on the line, and Max and Tess are running out of time.

Taste Me
By Cali Caliente

One impulsive tryst. One unforgettable fling.

Culinary columnist Aurora Daring adores creating desserts with fresh fruit and dreams of becoming a pastry chef. Always on the lookout for new food places to review, she visits Love's Farmer's Market, an old barn converted into a 'green store' with all the wonders a gourmet cook could possibly want. She finds something else as well—a ruggedly handsome man who fulfills all her sexual fantasies in one impromptu encounter.

Bryce Lovella loves his family's farm. His idea of expanding the farm to include a produce market is just the beginning of his aspirations. He also wants to start a family. When his twin brother, Brent, challenges him to find the perfect woman in two weeks' time and get her to say I love you, Bryce eagerly agrees to play. He's already seduced the woman of his dreams. There's only one problem—he never got her name.

Thank you for purchasing
this publication of The Wild Rose Press, Inc.

For questions or more
information contact us at
info@thewildrosepress.com.

The Wild Rose Press, Inc.
www.thewilderroses.com

To visit with authors of
The Wild Rose Press, Inc.
join our yahoo loop at
http://groups.yahoo.com/group/thewildrosepress/

www.ingramcontent.com/pod-product-compliance
Lightning Source LLC
Chambersburg PA
CBHW060941180626
46817CB00004B/1662